EYESTONE

D. R. MacDonald was born in Cape Breton, Nova Scotia, where his great-grandfathers were pioneers from the Highlands of Scotland. He spent most of his youth in Ohio and now teaches at Stanford University between visits to his land on Boularderie Island, Cape Breton. He was awarded a fellowship from the National Endowment for the Arts and his story "The Flowers of Bermuda" appeared in *Pushcart Prize XI*.

Creator of the world keep me sane,
Keep my sense and my wisdom, until you come for me.

SCOTTISH GAELIC SONG

EYESTONE

STORIES BY
D. R. MacDonald

A KING PENGUIN
PUBLISHED BY PENGUIN BOOKS

PENGUIN BOOKS
Published by the Penguin Group
Viking Penguin, a division of Penguin Books USA Inc.,
40 West 23rd Street, New York, New York 10010, U.S.A.
Penguin Books Ltd, 27 Wrights Lane,
London W8 5TZ, England
Penguin Books Australia Ltd, Ringwood,
Victoria, Australia
Penguin Books Canada Ltd, 2801 John Street,
Markham, Ontario, Canada L3R 1B4
Penguin Books (N.Z.) Ltd, 182–190 Wairau Road,
Auckland 10, New Zealand

Penguin Books Ltd, Registered Offices:
Harmondsworth, Middlesex, England

First published in the United States of America by Pushcart Press 1988
Published in Penguin Books 1989

1 3 5 7 9 10 8 6 4 2

The author is grateful to The National Endowment for the Arts for help
when he needed it, and to the Creative Writing Center of Stanford University for the friends he made there.

These stories originally appeared in the following publications: *Canto*
("Holy Annie"), *Southwest Review* ("Eyestone"), *The Sewanee Review*
("The Flowers of Bermuda"), *Sequoia* ("Work"), *TriQuarterly* ("Poplars"),
San Francisco Stories ("The Wharf King"), *Epoch* ("Of One Kind"), *The
Seattle Review* ("Sailing"). "The Flowers of Bermuda" was reprinted in
Pushcart Prize XI: Best of the Small Presses. Lyrics from "The Flowers of
Bermuda" by Stan Rogers.

Winner of the 1987 Editors' Book Award

Sponsoring editors for the Editors' Book Award are Simon Michael Bessie,
James Charlton, Peter Davison, Jonathan Galassi, David Godine, Daniel
Halpern, James Laughlin, Seymour Lawrence, Starling Lawrence, Robie
Macauley, Joyce Carol Oates, Nan A. Talese, Faith Sale, Ted Solotaroff, Pat
Strachan, Thomas Wallace. Nominating editor for this book: John Daniel.

LIBRARY OF CONGRESS CATALOGING IN PUBLICATION DATA
MacDonald, D. R.
Eyestone: stories/ by D. R. MacDonald.
p.   cm. — (King Penguin)
ISBN 0 14 01.2020 3
I. Title.
PR9199.3.M23E9   1989
813'.54—dc 19   88–34868

Printed in the United States of America
Set in Sabon
Designed by Mary Kornblum

FOR SHEILA AND ALEXIS,
WITH LOVE

Contents

EYESTONE

HOLY ANNIE

"He might've made something fine of his life," Rhoda MacCrimmon said to her sister.

Annie, whose lips had been moving daintily over the Psalms, lifted her eyes. "Yes, and handsome he was," she said, picking up her cue. "Smart as a whip."

"He loved rum more than living, and how many times did I tell him so." Rhoda stilled the tips of her knitting needles for an instant. "But those women, they were bad for him. They dragged him down."

"Dressed up, he looked professional. Like a doctor or a solicitor."

"Ah, he cut a figure, that man!"

The two women had sung this litany around their brother for so many years that to Annie its truth seemed as eternal as the verses under her fingertips. But Roder-

3

ick had been buried a week now, dead of heart failure. She wished there were more to say about him, that his final absence would have brought more than their old loving lamentations of him. No, it seemed that Roderick was said out, God rest his soul.

Rhoda glared at the misted kitchen window and then at the wall clock. "And where is that Dan Alex? His dad home three hours already." She was a florid woman and her plump face seemed to burn hotter at the mention of her son's name. "Had to come back without him, Angus did. How is that boy to get home from Sydney now, the last bus gone?"

"I suppose he'll hitchhike, dear," Annie said placidly. "He's a man, you know."

"Then he'll be a right soaked man." Her lips formed into a grouchy pout which as she gazed at her knitting dissolved into a faint affectionate smile. She lifted out of her lap the torso of a black sweater. "Was for him, this. Was for Roderick."

They both drew their breaths in a whisper of sadness. Then Rhoda's needles flashed faster among the strands of wool and Annie went back to her reading. But her eyes kept straying from the words tonight, fixing instead upon some mark on the page. A dark smudge. A nick in the paper's grain. The lacy stain of faded liquid. Had they happened in Africa? Who made them? She could not remember. The Bible, it seemed, had been with her since she was the girl who wanted to be a missionary. She had carried it everywhere, tucked in her arm like a wounded bird, quoting passages by heart. Behind her back they had called her Holy Annie and they shook their heads when the Presbyterian Church posted her to Ghana. She suffered thirteen months in the climate and then returned home to Cape Breton and her widowed dad. After his death she often crossed the fields to sit with Rhoda, and when the thin gossip of New Skye was exhausted she read her Bible, bending intensely over it as if her own life were recorded somewhere amongst the words. But this evening the lines flitted about like sparrows, settling nowhere in her mind.

From the bedroom overhead a snore rose and fell like the creaking timbers of a ship. Rhoda jammed her knitting down.

"Angus? Angus for the love of God stop that racket!" She cocked an ear until a loud snuffle shattered her husband's sleep. "Lord in heaven, he wakes the dead."

"He's tired out, dear. He had lots of errands in Sydney, tidying up Roderick's affairs and all."

"He didn't have to tidy up the tavern. That's one errand I didn't list."

"Now, it's not often he does that."

"Never's too often for me."

Annie sighed, blaming the day-long rain for a dismal feeling she could not shake. The wind was still out of the east, carrying in mist from the ocean that moved like vaporous airships slow and steady over the strait. She looked out at the last of a queer twilight glowing in the spirea bush by the window, its small white blossoms trembling beneath a leaky gutter. In the distance, streaks of hidden sun cut briefly through the smoky air along the ridge of the mountain, then they were smothered, and darkness settled fast. She was staring at the snow-white blossoms when she heard a thump at the back door followed quickly by an amiable curse. Dan Alec appeared in the dusk of the entryway, grinning widely under dripping hair.

"Sailor home from the sea," Rhoda said acidly to her sister, not looking at him. Her needles picked up speed.

"A sea of sorts," Dan Alec said roughly, then turned to his aunt. "Hullo, Annie. How're you t'day?"

"Fine, dear. We were worried a bit."

"No need. Ma likes to worry." Dan Alex crossed his arms and leaned against the doorframe regarding his mother with studied amusement. "Eh, Ma? What people think. That's her main worry."

"Talk nonsense, go ahead. All I might expect in that breeze of whisky blowing out your mouth."

"Rum, Ma. Uncle Rod's rum, matter of fact."

She stopped knitting and looked hard at him.

"Uncle Roderick is dead. Have some respect for him at least."

"I do, Ma, I do. More now than ever."

He winked at his aunt and swaggered into the kitchen. The rain had tightened his reddish hair into dense curls that made him look boyish in spite of his heavy features and the fisherman's squintlines around his eyes. A denim shirttail poked from the hem of his sweater, black like the one growing furiously beneath his mother's fingers. He raised the lid of the skillet and sniffed.

"Supper's cold and cold it'll stay," Rhoda said. "Your dad waited better than two hours for you."

"Then he wasted no time. Not in the Keltic Tavern he didn't."

"You're a pair, him snoring upstairs like a sick horse."

Ignoring her, Dan Alec lifted the skillet and spooned stew into his mouth. He weaved slightly as if the wind outside were moving him.

"Use a plate, for heaven's sake!" his mother hissed.

He paused in his chewing and narrowed his eyes at her. "I'll eat as I like."

"Not in this house you won't. You never have and you never will."

They stared each other down, Rhoda's back arched in her chair. Annie smiled between them. She was fond of her nephew and knew that Rhoda had been severe with him over the years. Oh, he had acted the devil more than once but there was nothing grave in it. She wished she had the power to end their bickering, and sometimes just her presence was enough, as if she were some sort of nun. But tonight their electricity arced over her.

Dan Alec set the skillet back on the stove. He rubbed his hands over the heat and then reached under his sweater as for a weapon, drawing out a pint of rum he'd tucked behind his buckle.

"Get rid of that!" his mother said sharply. "There's no liquor in this house!"

"You're after sounding like a sergeant, Ma, all rules and regulations." He held the bottle up to the light.

"Uncle Rod's. A bit of his legacy, eh? There's another one in his trashcan, empty. Now Dan Alec'll kill this one too, every drop. You wouldn't want me to chuck it out, not Uncle Rod's last pint."

Rhoda lay her hands in her lap as if to calm herself, but there was a tremor in her voice.

"What business had you in Roderick's house picking over his things? If Dad let you in, he had no right. It's to be shut up til it's sold."

Dan Alec took a tumbler from the cupboard and casually filled it with rum.

"Well, there's another has a key." He smiled at Annie as if she were in on the mystery, and she smiled innocently back.

"Who?" his mother demanded. "No one's to have a key but your Dad."

"Go easy, dear," Annie said, touching her arm. Rhoda's face was aflame. "Don't get excited so."

"Yes, Ma, go easy." Dan Alec gulped rum from the glass and wiped his mouth on his sleeve. "It's only Peg MacIvor what has a key."

"*Her?* That trash?"

Dan Alec inclined his head toward Annie. "Must excuse my mother, dear. The lady in question has always been 'that trash,' so far as Ma is concerned. Not respectable, no. Loose. She liked to drink and snuggle up with our Uncle Roderick. Of course he was fit only for a preacher's daughter."

Annie blushed and looked down at her Bible. Yes, she had now and then joined Rhoda in some headshaking over Peg MacIvor. Not that Annie had anything specific against the woman or knew much about her, only that she was the last in a string of them who had provided good company to her brother's bad habits. The few times he did stop drinking he had started up again, it seemed, as soon as another woman came along. . . .

"And what were *you* doing there with that woman, your uncle barely in his grave?"

"Nothing Uncle Rod would disapprove of, Ma. Nothing himself didn't do many's an evening."

"What would you know of his evenings?"

Dan Alec only grinned at her. She settled back in her chair and looked away as if she suddenly was afraid of an answer. Dan Alec was talking reckless, and there was Annie to consider.

"All I know is Peg MacIvor dragged him down like the rest," she said finally. "And that's a fact."

Annie thought back to the woman at the funeral, the one who'd stayed off to the side. She had looked haggard, too weary for a woman in her forties, even with a permanent fresh in her auburn hair. At the wake Rhoda would not speak to her, knowing Peg MacIvor had been with him when he was stricken. But Annie had felt a pang of sorrow for her. Sometimes she had tried to imagine Roderick with his women: her brother, for he was a soft-spoken man, sipping quietly on an iced drink in a dim room, the woman—any one of them—seated beside him talking loud and coarse. Beyond that she could not imagine his iniquities. But seeing that MacIvor woman in the shadows of the churchyard birches, Annie had imagined something quite different between them and felt a remorse she could not explain. And what had she known about his life, after all? Far less than this woman. Living twenty-five miles away he had kept it from her and from Rhoda except for the spare details that drifted like scraps of newspaper back to New Skye. When he did visit he listened patiently, a slight smile under his thin moustache as the sisters urged him to find a good wife. He would get up and look out the parlor window toward the Atlantic and say, "I miss the country. The air is better here." But as there was no liquor to be had in Rhoda's house, he would soon grow restless, kiss them goodbye and drive back to Sydney. Weeks would pass before they saw him but his name was forever coming up as if he had just stepped out the door. . . .

"That middle-aged tramp!" Rhoda's voice had risen to a shout that smothered what her son was saying.

Dan Alec moved to the table and set his rum in front of her. She swiped at the glass but he kept his grip on it and thumped it back down. "Now you listen to me, girl. Uncle Rod was down long before Peg MacIvor came by, and with women far worse. 'Give me a drinkin' lady anytime, Dan Alec,' he used to say. And you who thinks she knows every wicked corner in the county never got wind of his wild parties, day and night sometimes, four people to a bed the . . . "

"You're drunk and a liar!" Rhoda tried to rise but Dan Alec held her down by the shoulder.

"Drunk maybe, but no liar." He licked spilled rum from the back of his hand. "And here's more truth for you. I met Peg on Princes Street today. Some things led to others and off we went to Uncle Rod's place. We found his bottles quick enough, and we tumbled around in his bed besides. With his blessing, if I'm not mistaken."

"You dirt!"

"That man had a cock this long, Ma." Dan Alec expanded his hands like a fisherman sizing his catch. "And he was tuckin' it in the day he died."

From upstairs came a loud bark of laughter that seemed to vibrate through every room in the house. As if punched in the midriff Annie let out her held breath in a short cry and slowly closed her Bible. Rhoda shouted at the ceiling, "You shut up, Angus MacCrimmon! Laugh at this son of yours! Yes, you're a pair, the two of you!" But her voice was hoarse and distraught. She pushed damp strands of hair from her brow and looked beseechingly at her sister. "Oh, Annie, do you see what a torment he is! Thank the Lord he's the last child home and not the first or I'd never had another, and me giving him all I could . . ."

"Lord Jesus!" Dan Alec bawled. "You gave me the back of your hand!" His mother sank into her chair. Her breast heaved as she fought for words to combat him, her eyes angry and bright with tears.

"But that's all passed," he said evenly as he stood over her.

"This is my house too and I'll stay in it. You rail at Dad, if he'll take it. But leave Dan Alec alone."

He went into the adjoining parlor and stretched out on the sofa, propping his boots insolently on the armrest. Annie patted her sister's hand. She pitied her,

Rhoda looked so dazed, but she was not sure what comfort to give. True, Dan Alec had no right to be so crude but he had too long been treated like a misbehaving boy. Men were rough sometimes, and they had to have their bluster.

"He shouldn't have talked that dirt, you sitting in the middle of it," Rhoda said, wiping her eyes in her apron.

"Never mind, dear. I'm not a child in a white Sunday dress."

Angus's snoring had resumed full volume, rising and falling under the slow swells of his dreams. The rain had quit. The roof gutter leaked its last drops like ticks of a clock. In the parlor Dan Alec chuckled and then sighed with exaggerated contentment. "Uncle Rod indeed," he said loud enough to be heard in the kitchen. "By Jesus, that was a tough act to follow!"

His mother picked up her knitting from the floor and got to her feet slowly, agedly, cradling the balled wool up to her breast.

"I'll listen to no more of him!" she whispered fiercely to her sister. Annie could not recall her ever whispering in this kitchen, about anything. "Forgive me, dear, I'm going upstairs."

"Yes, you go rest. This won't be so bad in the morning."

"Not that I'll sleep, no, not with what I've put up with today. Will you take the path home, dear? Use the flashlight, won't you, and be careful, the ground is wet."

"I'll be fine, dear. Don't be too hard on Dan Alec. He's a young man yet."

"No, Annie. Right this hour he's as old as he'll ever be. Never change a hair of him." She stared into the parlor where his wet rubber boots shone in the light of the table lamp. "Oh, he'll go gray, yes, gray and sodden and snoring like his father. But what he is now he is for all his life." Pausing in the little hallway she looked back at her sister. "He could have been someone important, he really could have, you know."

"Who, dear?"

"Could take him for the prime minister in his dark blue suit. Sixty-one and a full head of hair, dark and wavy. . . ."

"Yes, dear. He was a bonny man."

Annie listened to her sister's heavy steps marking the stairs. The snoring had stopped. Murmurs, loud, then soft, played about the ceiling. The bed creaked deeply and the house was quiet again. Annie felt quite alone, more than she did in her own empty house. The evening had swirled around her and here she was rooted in the chair with her Bible. She looked around the kitchen helplessly. It was such a man's place. The work clothes of father and son hung on hooks by the stove. They gave off a faint smell of damp and sweat and warm rubber. Two hunting rifles were propped in a corner like brooms and a heap of stubbed-out cigarettes rested among the coal in the scuttle. Funny how Roderick was so different, elegant almost, even though he worked at the steel mill. Yet she remembered his eyes, how they looked his last visit: as if he were tired of sight.

She opened the Bible whose pages had so often

filled her loneliness. Leafing slowly through the Psalms she settled on the Nineteenth. Only her lips moved at first, then her soft voice she had read to her dad in, ". . . Day to day pours forth speech, and night to night declares knowledge. There is no speech nor are there words; their voice is not heard; yet their voice goes out through all the earth, and their words to the end of the world. . . ." But the verses did not soothe her and she closed the well-thumbed pages, the black cover smooth and stained from her hands in Africa. She recalled that place now like a hot light she had squinted into day after day without comprehension.

In the parlor, smoke from Dan Alec's cigarette crept into the air. He was clapping his boots together slowly like hands. "Damn," he said aloud but to himself, "I'm not sure if she was laughin' or cryin'."

Annie sat looking at the glass of rum. She took it in her hands gently like an antique vase and turned it around and around, finally shutting her eyes as she sipped from the rim. A harsh warmth shuddered through her. She ran her tongue slowly over her lips: this is what women tasted on her brother. She remembered that his words were tinged with this sour-sweetness when he said close to her face, "See you in a while, Annie, dear." He had always been kind.

She listened to Dan Alec's slow breathing in the next room. She wanted to go in and talk to him, but what would she say? For much of her life she had dealt out bits of the Bible, if diffidently, more often to herself than to others. Now her mind roamed chapter and verse in vain. There was no comfort, no hope in the way she felt in this kitchen. If she walked into that other room and her nephew looked up at her he would think, though he wouldn't speak it, "Holy Annie," and then they both would have to talk in a certain way. She did not want that. She wanted to ask him something that might surprise him, that he would never expect from this woman who always had a Bible open before her as if it spoke all her mind and heart.

But standing at the door to the parlor she saw Dan Alec asleep, his cigarette fagging out in a saucer. He looked so harmless now, susceptible, merely a man. She crushed out the cigarette and returned to the kitchen.

After tidying up for Rhoda she put on her tan raincoat and tied a plastic scarf carefully around her hair. Then she noticed the rum in the center of the table. Without hesitation she seized the glass and raised it quickly to her lips, drinking what was left in a long swallow. There. That was the last of it. Heat swelled like a wave through her body and she reeled backwards against the wall. Giddy, she was. Heat always made her giddy and faint. Her eyes blurred with tears and her hands trembled like strummed wires but she gathered up the Bible and felt her way out the back door into a cool damp darkness. The rum wasn't so bad, once the fire died. It seemed to be melting now into her limbs, lightening them. A soft mist fanned her flushed cheeks. She smiled up at the sky. The wind had gone round to the west and was ferrying great clouds toward the sea. Moving fast, they rolled enormous over the ridge, an unseen moon writhing white in the gauzy spaces among them. More awesome than spaceships, they were, churning so silently, and where were they going? "The heavens are telling the glory of God," she whispered, and she realized she was laughing as if someone had told her a joke in her sleep. She clapped a hand to her mouth for this silliness, swaying wide-eyed now in hay to her waist. The path home ran like a dark stream through the old pasture. The grasses parted and closed as though under a sea, languid and waved with shadows. She waded toward the woods out of whose branches blew a rich smell of balsam. Everything was in motion, it seemed, for her, for Annie, even though the old footpath was narrow that had once been wide enough for two. Only a trickle of feet now drip drip to her door. Her coat had come open and her dress was getting wet but she didn't care. She remembered walking out in Africa through tall grass one early morning, the dew so heavy she raised her skirt, but the grasses, cool against her skin, had soaked her stockings through. . . . Startled that she was so suddenly face down in sodden stalks of hay, she got up with difficulty and set her eyes again for home. But her hands felt light and she stopped to ponder. Her Bible. Couldn't go on without that, no. She went back a few steps and knelt where her body had pressed down the hay. The Bible was slippery with damp and she rubbed her hands over it. Hadn't it seen worse weathers though? Terrible suns, and rains to drown you? She sang now as she walked but the words made no sense. Oh this was nice whatever it was, turning her around and around with a fistful of clover. Any direction would do when you spun like a top. No need rushing, and nobody waiting besides. Dad had rum hidden somewhere, that she knew. She would search for it tonight. Fun to swing from room to room, turning out trunks and cupboards, then finding it, a secret. Did Rod do that ever? Dan Alec did, and shame on him too. When she neared the stand of spruce that divided her dad's land from MacCrimmon's, she looked up at the black trees. What if she had lost her Bible here? Didn't she know this meadow like the veins on her hand, all its crossings and crisscrossings? She would have found it in the morning. Like the stones in the field it would be waiting. . . .

EYESTONE

He does not understand why an old widow need wash every sheet she owns. Her men are gone—her sons, her husband. But there is much about Mrs. Corbett he does not understand. Sometimes when he strolled through the pasture, rich with wildflowers he sought to identify, he could feel her watching from behind the kitchen curtains and he would flush with anger. How was it she could make him feel like a trespasser? He wants to shout, that's *my* house you're standing in. But she is old. Sometimes in the woods he glimpses her as she forages for plants: suddenly she is there, and then not. She is a folk healer, or was. She takes her clothesbasket into the house, looking his way once before she closes the door. Is it callous to think she might die to oblige him? Maybe Royce's wife was right: Mrs. Corbett will outlive everything.

Even inside the barn Royce can feel her eyes. Nearly a year has passed since her husband, from the milkcan in the middle of the threshing floor, took his last step into space. From the high vaulted ceiling the hayfork sways almost imperceptibly like a rung bell coming to rest. Poor devil. He barely knew the man, but during the first months after Royce purchased the farm, old Corbett sat propped on his cot in the kitchen, staring out the east window at the weather, at the barn he built himself, the last of its red paint scoured away in salt winds and the driven ice of storms. The day Royce brought the papers around for him to sign, Mrs. Corbett, whispering to herself in Gaelic, sat glumly in one corner of the parlor as if her husband were selling not the land but her. Nonetheless, Corbett extracted from

Royce the promise that she be allowed to live on in the house until her death—a concession Royce gladly granted, wanting only the land at that time, others being after it. "The cottage across the road will do for myself, and my wife," Royce said. "When she joins me." A rash statement, but perhaps rashness characterized everything he'd done since he met that woman, that girl. Corbett, obviously ill, pointed to the ceiling: "Upstairs there, my mother and my dad died, in the same year. No running water then, and we nursed them all that long time they were sick. You'll never see me in a hospital, or my wife either."

Afterward, Royce gave Corbett hardly a thought, absorbed as he was in his hundred acres of woods, fields, and shore. He did not know that Corbett was sitting out his nights in the kitchen struggling for breath, sleeping in fits and snatches with his chin on his breast, or that sometimes his wife fixed a strand of red yarn around his neck. And then one warm morning when the untilled fields burgeoned with hay and flowers and weeds, Corbett, his wife away in town, hobbled out to the barn and hung himself in a loop of the hayfork rope, swinging from a ridgepole that bore the scars of his own axe.

On the planks of the threshing floor Royce tests his weight. A few have stove in, pattered into rot from leaks. "I'm going to make something new here, when the old lady is gone," he'd said to his wife not long after she arrived. A shingle or two have sloughed away, seams have spread some. Wind pries at the aluminum roofing, but the handhewn posts are solid, the beams and purlins true. He foresaw this barn, in his daydreams back in Boston, as a big lodge which, to bring in money, he might let out to artists in the summer, easterners seeking rural peace, and, since he was a painter himself, offer instruction even though he didn't want to teach anymore. It was one of several schemes he brought with him, and with which he passed his first winter here, sketching rooms and windows and furniture through dark housebound afternoons, showing to his wife their ever-increasing elaborateness as if the detail alone might counter her growing indifference. She chided him for not painting anymore, for giving up. "You might have noticed," he said, "there are no galleries around here." Her own pale but happy watercolors she'd filled her summer with turned into the harsh shades of late autumn, then into the loneliness of snow and cold. "This could be a hut in Labrador," she said one evening. "We have no friends. We're always running out of things, all kinds of things." He was stir-crazy too by then but determined not to go back to Boston, not yet. "We'll make this place ours, even in the winter," he said. She said, "Never. We're summer people, Royce. That's the part of you I loved." He told her no, you have to take the country in all seasons and that doesn't come easy. "Maybe you're too young for the country," he said. "I thought you could handle it." She looked at him. "Handle what? What are we handling?"

Spring came so late it was hardly spring at all, mid-May and shadowsnow still blue at the edge of the woods. "She has a fireplace down there," his wife said, looking out the window at Mrs. Corbett's house. Royce got up and stood behind her. "She comes with the place," he said. On the pane were fish spines of frost. After two days of wind and freezing rains, his wife packed and he drove her to the airport in Sydney. "It was a bad idea from the start, wasn't it?" she said. "For me?" He kissed her and stepped back, already missing her. "I guess I've used up my ideas," he told her. "I'll see this one through."

He pokes around the barn, touching things he owns but that never seem his. Rusting machinery lies forlornly about. Someday he'll paint them bright colors. A tooth harrow, a hayrake, the last harvest its graceful tines have gathered tumbling out of the lofts, bales broken, the mildewed hay scattered. He smells the dried manure in the raw, browned wood of the stalls: underneath their collapsed planks he once found a cow skull gaping from the soft earth and took it home to his wife who delighted in such objects. On a doorpost there is a dark sheen where Corbett's hand so many times took hold. When Royce is inside the barn, his careful, exact drawings seem to have no connection at all to it. The sharp warmth, the worn surfaces have an intimacy he longs to feel on canvas but cannot.

He turns to the milkcan and pushes it over with his foot. It crunches along the planks a short distance and stops. One afternoon he sketched her by the light of the back door, a fine dust rising from the dry hay and settling lightly on her skin, moist in the barn's heat, skin he can taste now, vividly. Overhead at the tiny gable window a swallow, defeated by glass, assails the dusty pane again and again. He tries to scare it out with stones from his pocket, pegging them at the roof, but the bird will not quit. Leaving, he props open the door so the swallow and its ill-luck can leave with him. In the barn's foundation there is a new crack. His wife would stoop and run her fingers over the small shells embedded in its concrete—periwinkles and snails, bits of scallop, oyster, clam.

Royce squints up at the white-grey sky. The sun burns somewhere. He can feel its heat, and for a moment a sudden aimlessness comes over him. He looks quickly at the fading white shingles of the house: a curtain moves in the kitchen.

It is with some weariness that he pushes himself into thickets that obliterate paths he found, or made, only the summer before, vowing then not only to draw everything on wings, legs, or roots but to learn their identities as well. Now heavy spring rains have left the meadows lush and soggy, sheer growth which, in June, swept green and rapid over the fields. Dense grass he stomped down is combed back by the wind as if he never passed there. In any case, his hikes have become more random, pointless, their only objective to eat up time before he must return to the cottage. As he moves through browntop grass, he trails his fingers in its kinky silk and smiles: it feels like her hair.

He follows a deer path into a sea of ferns, waist-high fronds that have raced into summer in the shade of birches, hiding stumps and deadfalls. Under them lies a humid ferny scent, warm when you fall into it, like under a skirt. His wife had hiked to places that did not attract him, and she would stay there drawing as long as blackflies and the weather allowed. Her landscapes, though never from a perspective he would have chosen, he praised despite their lack of risk, their melodrama. The rattling croak of a raven passes overhead. "Corvus corax," Royce whispers. He had recited her the Latin names of things they encountered. Most of the birds he could recognize now, having offered themselves easily in the spring, bits of color in the dun days of dead hay and bare trees but now just teasing sounds in the leaves. He speaks the names of flowers as he walks. "Achillea millefolium. Eupatorium perfoliatum. Aletris farinosa. Prunella vulgaris." He rolls the Latin on his tongue, but Mrs. Corbett would know them by their common names—yarrow, boneset, heal-all, colicroot—evoking broken limbs, fevers, writhing infants. And yet one windy afternoon last summer, taking them to his wife, he approached Mrs. Corbett holding out a cluster of what he now knew as spotted touch-me-nots. Bundled in her late husband's tattered sweater and seated on a milking stool, its legs trussed with wire, she had continued slicing seed potatoes for her little plot. "Goldenrod," she said, barely glancing. "No," he said. "Even I know goldenrod." She tossed the bad part of a potato into a battered pail, the good into a basket. "There's some here that wasn't here before," she said finally, never looking at him. "She draws flowers. Ask your wife." Royce bid her good day, and before he reached the cottage door, the blooms were withered petals of orange and red.

Feeling rank with repellant and sweat, he squats down by the purling coolness of a brook. He remembers his wife trying to sketch him here. "I can never do you," she said, scowling him over with scribbles. It was true. Her drawings of him were always off the mark, as if she were unwilling to see what he really looked like.

Before he raises his head, he knows that Mrs. Corbett is there, somewhere up among the trees. Just above a bend in the ravine, she is working her hand over the trunk of a fir, stroking its bark for pitch. Her white hair stands out against the needled branches and she holds a pint basket. If she is aware of him she gives no sign. She is singing in a soft, cooing rill a Gaelic song he has heard her sing before, "*Tha mo chúl riut, Tha mo chúl riut. . . .*" Is it some charm for gathering balsam, for urging sap from the tree? Often he has come across her trail, sometimes no more than a faint cleavage through fern, a cloudy footprint in brookside mud. When he looks up again she is gone.

My wife, he thinks, is with another man now. A new teacher.

The brook disappears into a marsh which he skirts to reach the nearly sandless shore (a disappointment to his wife who liked beaches). Its short slope is strewn with large rounded stones, and when the east wind blows up a storm you can hear their liquid clack and rumble under the spreading foam. He kicks over driftwood as he goes. A cormorant, straining its reptilean neck, skims the grey sea toward the Bird Islands, bleak tables in the distance. He tugs at a lobster trap partly buried in the sand until the old manila line snaps. He still reaches for gifts on his hikes, even though his wife has left, and he takes them home—a broken antler, a shed snakeskin, the intact skeleton of a cat he lifted bone by bone from a bed of moss. He pockets two spikes that have rusted together and climbs a short bank, pushing his way through the spruce. A bird, one he's been after for months, calls somewhere above him, but as he fumbles for the glasses a held branch slips and strikes him in the face. Hunched and swearing he touches his eye, but the wet is tears, not blood. He protects it with his arm and beats aside the tough spruce until he reaches an old path that leads up to Mrs. Corbett's lower pasture. The pain subsides but something scratches at his eyeball, a bit of needle or bark. A narrow stream crosses the path and he kneels beside it, scooping water over his face, wincing. "You saw this place in your dreams, Royce," his wife said. "Nothing will come of that barn down there. And that house. You're not even a painter anymore. All you have are plans on paper." What did she know, really? That he was only reaching from one handhold to the next?

The path opens out into a rise and he gets his bearings from the barn roof, from its weathervane made of handsawn boards. Skewed by the wind, it resembles some species of drunken fowl, leaning north, pointing east. He breaks off a maple sapling to whisk away the flies.

Mrs. Corbett appears along the ridge of haytops above him, first her head, then her shoulders as she crosses from the barn. On other afternoons he has seen her on that path, a kerchief clasped to her chin, her gait slow and absorbed as if she were returning from church. He does not know what she does in there. Stand where her husband died perhaps, conjure him. Telling his wife about his plans, Royce had always prefaced them by saying, "When the old lady leaves. . . ." But one day in that wintry spring his wife cut him short: "Mrs. Corbett isn't going anywhere. That's like saying, wait until the trees leave, wait until the rocks go away." Suddenly his irritation converges upon her—the pain in his eye, the itch and sweat of tramping his own land with nothing to show for it but a solitary meal and another night in a cottage. If he takes the house, she will be gone.

When he shouts her name the air seems to smother his voice. But she stops and turns. The nearer he gets to her, the less certain he is as to how he will put it. She stands calmly on the pathway as he staggers through the ripe hay. He wonders if she has looked like this always, gaunt, straight, her eyes pale as beach shells. He has tried to sketch her in the past, but always at a distance or from memory, the versions as varied as his moods.

"Listen," he says. His eye squints tears. "There's this . . . this bird, Mrs. Corbett. I hear it all the time. Just after dark even." When he can draw a good breath he whistles a reasonable imitation of its call.

"The Bridal Bird, is what my sister Mary used to call it," she says.

"I've never heard of that one."

"She was a little foolish, my sister." Mrs. Corbett pulls the flowered scarf off her head and tucks it into her hands. Her hair is very white and he feels dizzied by it. The rims of his eye tremble.

anymore. Even his good eye is getting sore from the strain. And evicting the old lady bothers him. She and her husband, they courted in buggy and sleigh. He squints glumly at clouds low to the sea, a bluish ridge streaked like agate from the sun where a storm is building over the water, clouds bruising and swelling. Lightning blinks harmlessly in the distance. In the rising wind the cottage crackles like ice, the air suddenly cool in the room. He and his wife had laughed that summer—nervously at first—about the tickings and creakings, lying wide-eyed in bed while the stairs released sounds of footsteps stored in their wood. Under the covers they joked about ghosts, about the retired minister who'd died here, and then made love, safe in its heat. But they kept a lamp burning downstairs throughout the nights until they were used to the profoundly quiet darkness, so deep the whole world might be dark.

He hears the bird again, far away, fainter as it shelters from the coming storm. Whitecaps leap and flicker in the sea, and though the woods behind Mrs. Corbett's barn hide the shore, he knows waves are beginning to break and reach, stirring the beach stones. He wipes the sticky dampness from his cheek. The eye throbs. Too late now to find a doctor. He can't drive through rain with his sight cut in two. Her house darkens against the wild fields, the swaying trees. Three weeks ago he flew to Boston to see his wife. There was a look to her he hadn't seen in a long time. She had resumed graduate study, but was now praising a potter, a talented and crazy man ten years her senior (drunk, he'd crawled across the floor at a party, removed one of her sandals,

and caressed her foot with kisses) though not too crazy
to be tenured. Ceramics, she told Royce, was what she
needed all along, their tactility, their sensuousness.
Around her apartment sat free-form pots, organic, sug-
gestive. Royce begged off a party they'd been invited to,
so she went alone. Sitting in the dark, he called up an
old colleague, a man he'd knocked around with, but the
man's fires were all banked now, his affairs behind him,
and he talked as if Royce were calling from Antarctica.
After Royce hung up, there was no one else he cared to
talk to. Late at night in the cottage he and his wife had
listened to the marine weather report just to hear the
flow of the names . . . Bay of Fundy, Banqero Bank,
Sable Island, Fourchu, East Scotia Slope, Cabot Strait,
Gulf Magdalen, Anticosti . . . seas two to four
feet. . . . He had come to Cape Breton, so he'd
thought, for a last chance to find something original in
himself. But he had come as well to keep a woman, to
sustain her ardor. Hadn't his break with the past im-
pressed her at first, the very gesture of it? But it was
only his past he'd broken from, not hers. And in that
setting, she came to appraise him differently. He had
nothing more to teach her, only more to learn. The next
morning while she slept, he left her apartment and flew
back to Sydney.

And now he owns this land. Does he not? He has
not stolen it. Didn't they let so much of their land slip
away, these people, let it go to so many strangers like
himself that even the government got alarmed? Dead
farms, and distant indifferent heirs selling out to Americans, Western Canadians, Germans, whoever had the

cash. Not Mrs. Corbett. He raises his rum to her, and drinks.

But Mrs. Corbett, have I not risked a great deal? I chucked a college job, cashed my pension. I *left* Boston, left that place your kin fled to over the generations, the Boston States, land of plenty. I was forty. Do you remember that age? Did you fret over it? I fell in love. I thought what I needed was to be foolish. I swept her away into the country. Country? What did we know? There were drives through rural landscapes on autumn Sundays, through those miracles of leaves. And on that summer trip to Cape Breton, even the bad weather looked good to us. I subscribed to a country magazine and looked at pictures of people burning wood in Swedish stoves and getting endeared to draft horses and goats. Maybe I should have arrived on horseback, Mrs. Corbett. I couldn't have come less prepared, or more deluded. But no one could have told me how you pass the hours here, or what a truly dark night is like, even with a woman sleeping in your arms, her watercolors taped to the walls.

He touches his eye: gritty, inflamed. He'll need to finish the rum before he sleeps. He glances at the cat skull under the lamp, its cheekbones flaring like small wings. Wind cracks sharply in the walls. Across the road Mrs. Corbett's kitchen has become a solitary veil of light, and east of it the metal roof of the barn shines with rain. There'd be a wind blowing through the rafters now, scattering hay, tolling the hayfork. Is the swallow roosting or is it free?

Rain hits sudden and hard, peppering the window-pane. Sears of lightning strike the sea, their tendrils bright, and he tenses for thunder. It comes, like stone splitting. In its wake the radio quits and the tablelamp winks out. He gets up and feels for a wall switch. Nothing. A good Cape Breton blackout. That could last for hours. He moves his chair further back from the window which has begun to leak as it always does when windward. He fetches towels and applies them to the sill, wringing them out and replacing them as if the house has a fever. He holds one, chilly with rain, against his face. Remembering a bedroom, he runs upstairs to the single gabled room where a wet curtain slaps against the wall and slams the window shut. Lightning flares off the white canvasses strewn about. Mrs. Corbett's house has been reduced to the rain-hazy glow of her kitchen. She'd be using candles or kerosene now. But his unlit cottage is soothing and he likes the sounds of the storm. Recalling from his youth rules for survival, he stands back from the window. Don't shelter under trees. Don't court a lightning bolt with your nose to a windowpane. He could add another to that list now: don't love a young woman, and don't take her to a place like this. Ah, but Mrs. Corbett, she has survived hazards and dangers. She knows about ailments far more grave than a bit of bark in the eye. She has washed her own dead for burial. That she used leaves and resins to make medicine Royce knows from old Hector who keeps a store at the highway. And that she tried to save her husband with a salve she rubbed at night into his ribs. "A blood charmer, the best—seventh daughter of a seventh son," Hector said. "She can stop you bleeding with just your name, just the saying of it." She once healed a festering foot that Hector wounded on a two-handed scythe. Hector believes in her cures—a coin to ease the agony of diseased bone, a drawing poultice, healing water from a hidden spring. From his cottage last summer Royce saw occasional visitors come, all elderly. But this year none. Maybe her husband's death has sapped her powers, or left a pall.

Downstairs, he works away at the rum, his back to the wall. Thunder passes into rumbles further west but the rain stays heavy. His eye clenches like a hot fist. The woods will be cool now, taking in the sea. He goes outdoors and turns his face up to the rain. In the gravel of the driveway a large toad leaps with a sound like a tossed beanbag. He is used to them now. They can bring luck, Hector says, but somehow you must extract, without killing them, their potent bones—one like a fork, the other a spoon. Do you know the secret of that, Mrs. Corbett? He presses his palm to his face: the eye beats like a heart.

He feels his way back inside and begins to pull wildflowers from bottles and jars arranged on the windowsills. He stuffs charcoal sticks into his pocket and shelters the bouquet under a sketchpad as he crosses the road to her house. The barn is a dim stain in the mist that streams and eddies around him. The back door opens to his knock and she is there in the faint light of the kitchen.

"It's for your eye you're here," she says.

He cannot find in her voice any suggestion of how she feels. Scorn, pity, indifference—any of them are possible.

"Come inside then." She holds the screendoor open and waits.

It's been a long time since he was in her house, and never at night. The silence seems fixed under the steady rain. There is a smell of ashes from the stove. An old kerosene lamp, a hairline crack in its chimney, burns on the table, and under its soft white light are set two china dishes. The small bowl, its glaze patterned with bluebells, holds something like sugar, the matching saucer a liquid, water perhaps. She goes into the pantry and comes back with a towel which she hands to him. He rubs it over his face and thanks her.

"I don't mind the rain, to tell you the truth," he says.

She stares at his fistful of ragged flowers.

"For you." He fluffs them with his fingers, the purple loosestrife, the closed blooms of hawkweed. "They used to think this gave hawks their sharp sight. But probably you knew that. Probably your husband called it devil's paintbrush."

"It doesn't matter now," she says. "Nice of you to bring them." She takes the flowers and puts them into a canning jar on the table. She points to the threadbare cot by the east window where on the tartan blanket her husband dozed and sat out his last months. "You lie there."

"No, I only came down for candles, Mrs. Corbett. And to draw you. I want to draw your portrait."

"Oh, there'll be no pictures of me, and this is no kind of light for doing them."

He cannot see her face clearly, as he had not that afternoon Corbett signed over the land. He feels oddly helpless and tired. He sits on the very edge of the cot, listening to the storm revive, the tremors of thunder in the roof.

"No, I'll drive to the doctor tomorrow," he says. "It's nothing. I was careless in the woods. I deserved it."

But her long thin hands are moving under the lamplight, lifting some object from the bowl. She puffs on it, then rinses it in the saucer. She bears it carefully toward him between finger and thumb. It looks like a tiny white pebble.

"You've come to where the eyestone is," she says. "It cannot travel but in the eye. Lie back now. Let the stone work."

"I don't think I need this," he says, trying to rise, but she presses him down. When she lifts his eyelid, he sucks in his breath and grips her by the wrist, releasing it as she lowers the lid over the stone.

"What is it?" he whispers. Yet he can barely feel it.

"Lie still. You mustn't move about. Let the stone move. It's very old in my family, the stone, very old."

"I have to get back to the cottage. I can't stay."

"Not much to be done in the dark," she says.

"I have a lot to do. But listen . . . "

"You can't do what you can't see."

"Listen, Mrs. Corbett. You don't have to leave the house. Stay. Stay as long as you like."

"I have done that," she says. She seats herself by the table, her back to the lamp. He cannot remember what she looks like. Just her white hair, her freckled hands. A key hangs on a nail above the cot. Attached to it with a bit of red yarn is a crudely whittled bird, its wings spread as in flight. Tired, he begins to talk, afraid of sleep.

"There's a tribe somewhere, in Sumatra, I think," he says. "They cut effigies of birds out of wood, with their machetes. They carve a body and soaring wings. The souls of these people are always flying, and now they have to beckon them home or they'll fly too far away and die. They hang the wooden birds up high on poles, to draw their souls back home. . . ." He smiles. "Forgive me. I used to be a teacher. It was your weather-vane I was thinking of. . . ."

"It shows the wind different now."

He poises his hand above his eye but refrains from touching it. The stone is there. But soft, cool.

"Tell me what this is, Mrs. Corbett."

She waits until a run of thunder has bowled through the house, shivering windowpanes and the lamp. The cot gives off an old smell of tobacco.

"The very tip of a conch," she says. "So my father told me. But even to him it was old, carried and cared for since a long time. Nobody knows where it came from, or where it will go. It's alive. It knows the eye."

Rain sweeps over the window like hail. He raises his head. "How long?"

She motions him still.

"I can't sleep here," he says. "Don't let me sleep."

"She's not coming back, is she. Your wife."

He sits up and looks at her. He lies slowly back.

"The bird you're after finding," she says. "It would be a white-throated sparrow, from the sound of it."

"A sparrow? I'd hoped for something grander." He closes his eyes. "I've heard you singing sometimes. What words are they? What do they mean?"

She shifts in her chair. "Just the song of a bird."

"But they're words, aren't they? Don't they say something?"

"They say, 'My back to you, My back to you . . . You're not of my kin. . . .' It's only a song that pigeons make. The birds knew Gaelic once."

The rain has come back heavy. It sings over the windows.

"Were you pretty, Mrs. Corbett, when you were young?"

She touches her cheekbone, then lays her hand out flat on the table. "Some thought so," she says. "But you get weathered. There's no shelter from that."

The wind coos in the stove flue. She is standing beside him.

"Royce Simmons," she says. "The house is yours."

He turns his head and glimpses the flowers, drooping from their journey in the rain. But Mrs. Corbett is gone. The kitchen has a final tidiness about it, everything arranged and at rest. "Mrs. Corbett?" His voice drifts into the recesses of the house. . . .

He feared it would press like a stone, the eye so tender, but instead it meanders softly, caressing the inflamed flesh like the mouth of a snail as it slips through his dream. He is climbing a stairway at night but the going is hard, slow. He lugs a pail and its weight staggers him, the water soaking his feet as he struggles up toward the landing. From some upstairs room an old man calls out for a drink of water, and then a woman too, their cries mingling into a single terrifying sound. He is afraid to find their rooms in the dark, their neatly made beds. He fears their faces are white as moons. Fever is in the air, it is hard to breathe and he wants to wake. He dips his hand into the bucket but the water too is warm. A woman's mouth closes on his own, sliding away. In the pungeant warmth of the barn, hay and flowers, withered and stiff, rustle under his steps. The barn seems so huge and high with light streaming like rain through the open rafters. He stands over the threshing floor, fixed by an eye, small, a bird's, a white throat beating like an artery. He wants to take it in his hands, feel it there viscous, but instead the coarse scratch of hemp constricts him and his mouth widens. The warped boards of the weathervane reel in the wind. The rope is red, he knows it is red though he cannot see it, and when the bird, its wings beating, moves for his eye in the dark of the hayloft, he falls away into the grass. In the deep grass someone bends to him and she holds the bone like a spoon and he must drink from it, taste the tears that burn in his eye. When the spoon touches his lips, he turns away, but the taste is sweet like water from a spring.

THE
FLOWERS
OF BERMUDA

IN MEMORY OF M. D. M.

Bilkie Sutherland took the postcard from behind his rubber bib and slowly read the message one more time: "I'm going here soon. I hope your lobsters are plentiful. My best to Bella. God bless you. Yours, Gordon Mac-Lean." Bilkie flipped it over: a washed out photograph in black and white. *The Holy Isle. Iona. Inner Hebrides.* On the land stood stone ruins, no man or woman anywhere, and grim fences of cloud shadowed a dark sea. So this was Iona.

"You want that engine looked at?" Angus Carmichael, in his deepwater boots, was standing on the wharf above Bilkie's boat.

"Not now. I heard from the minister."

"MacLean?"

"He's almost to Iona now."

Angus laughed, working a toothpick around in his teeth. "Man dear, *I've* been to Iona, was there last Sunday." Angus meant where his wife was from, a Cape Breton village with a Highland museum open in the summer, and a St. Columba Church.

"It's a very religious place," Bilkie said, ignoring him. "Very ancient, in that way."

"Like you, Bilkie."

"I'm the same as the rest of you."

"No, Bilkie. Sometimes you're not. And neither is your Reverend MacLean."

Angus's discarded toothpick fluttered down to the deck. Bilkie picked it up and dropped it over the side. Angus never cared whether his own deck was flecked with gurry and flies. Nor was he keen on Gordon MacLean. Said the man was after putting in a good word for the Catholics. But that wasn't the minister's point at all. "We're all one faith, if we go back to Iona," is what he'd said. And nothing much more than that.

As Bilkie laid out his gear for the next day's work, he heard singing. No one sang around here anymore. Radios took care of that. He stood up to listen. Ah! It was Johnny, Angus's only boy, home from Dalhousie for the summer. He had a good strong voice, that boy, one they could use over at the church. But you didn't see him there, not since college. No singer himself, Bilkie could appreciate a good tune. His grandfather had worked the schooners in the West Indies trade, and Johnny's song had the flavor of that, of those rolling vessels . . . " 'He could smell the flowers of Bermuda in

the gale, when he died on the North Rock Shoal. . . .' "
Bilkie stared into the wet darkness underneath the
wharf where pilings were studded with snails. Algae
hung like slicked hair on the rocks. He had saved Gordon MacLean under that wharf, when the man was just
a tyke. While hunting for eels, Gordon had slipped and
fallen, and Bilkie heard his cries and came down along
the rocks on the other side to pull him out, a desperate
boy clutching for his hand.

Bilkie's car, a big salt-eaten Ford, was parked at the
end of the wharf, and whenever he saw it he wished
again for horses who could shuck salt like rain. At
home the well pump had quit this morning and made
him grumpy. He'd had to use the woods, squat out
there under a fir, the birds barely stirring overhead, him
staring at shoots of Indian Pipe wondering what in hell
they lived on, leafless, white as wax, hardly a flower at
all. Up by the roadside blue lupines were a little past
their prime. What flowers, he wondered, grew on Iona?

The car swayed through rain ruts, past clumps of
St. Johnswort (*allas Colmcille* his grandfather had
called them) that gave a wild yellow border to the driveway. His house appeared slowly behind a corridor of
tall maples. In their long shade red cows rested. Sometimes everything seemed fixed, for good. His animals,
his life. But God had taken away his only boy, and
Bilkie could not fathom that even yet. For a time he had
kept sheep, but quit because killing the lambs bothered
him.

Bella was waiting at the front door, not the back,

her palm pressed to her face. He stopped shy of the porch, hoping it wasn't a new well-pump they needed.

"What's wrong?"

"Rev. MacLean's been stabbed in Oban," his wife said, her voice thin.

Bilkie repeated the words to himself. There was a swallows nest above the door. The birds swooped and clamored. "Not there?" he said. "Not in Scotland?" A mist of respect, almost of reverence, hovered over the old country. You didn't get stabbed there.

"Jessie told me on the phone, not a minute ago. Oh, he'll live all right. He's living."

Over supper Bella related what she knew. Gordon MacLean had been walking in Oban, in the evening it was, a woman friend with him. Two young thugs up from Glasgow went for her handbag, right rough about it too. Gordon collared one but the other shoved a knife in his back.

"He's not a big man either," Bilkie said, returning a forkful of boiled potato to his plate. He had known Gordon as a child around the wharf, a little boy who asked hard questions. He had pulled him from the water. He'd seen him go off to seminary, thinking he would never come back to Cape Breton, not to this corner of it, but after awhile he did. To think of him lying in blood, on a sidewalk in Oban. "Did they catch the devils?"

"They did. He'll have to testify."

"What, go back there?"

"When he's able. Be a long time until the trial."

Bilkie felt betrayed. A big stone had slipped somehow out of place. Certain things did not go wrong there, not in the Islands where his people came from. Here, crime was up, too few caring about a day's work, kids scorning church. Greedier now, more for themselves, people were. But knives, what the hell. There in the Hebrides they'd worked things out, hadn't they, over a long span of time? It had seemed to him a place of hard wisdom, hard won. Not a definite place, for he had never been there, but something like stone about it: sea-washed, nicely worn, and high cliffs where waves whitened against the rocks. He knew about the Clearances, yes, about the bad laws that drove his grandfather out of Lewis where he'd lived in a turf house. But even then they weren't knifing people. Gordon MacLean, a minister of God, couldn't return there and come to no harm? To Mull first he'd been headed, to MacLean country. And then to Iona, across a strait not much wider than this one. But a knife stopped him in Oban, a nice sort of town by the sea.

From his parlor window Bilkie could see a bit of the church in the east, the dull white shingles of its steeple above the dark spruce. *We all have Iona inside us,* the man had said. *Our faith was lighted there.* Why then did this happen?

Bilkie had asked such a question before and found no answer. They'd had a son, he and Bella, so he knew about shock, and about grief. Even now, thinking of his son and the schoolhouse could suck the wind right out of him. The boy was born late in their lives anyway, and maybe Bilkie's hopes had come too much to rest in him. Was that the sin? Torquil they called him, an old name out of the Hebrides, after Bella's dad. But one October afternoon when the boy was nine, he left the schoolhouse and forgot his coat, a pea coat, new, with a big collar turned up like a sailor's. So he went back to get it, back to the old white schoolhouse where he was learning about the world. It was just a summer house now, owned by strangers. But that day it was locked tight, and the teacher gone home. A young woman. No blame to her. His boy jimmied open the window with his knife. They were big, double-hung windows, and you could see them open yet on a warm weekend, hear people drunk behind the screens. But Torquil had tried to hoist himself over the sill, and the upper half of the window unjammed then and came down on his neck. Late in the day it was they found him, searching last the grounds of the school. A time of day about now. The sash lay along his small shoulders like a yoke, that cruel piece of wood, blood in his nose like someone had punched him. . . .

Bilkie barely slept. He was chased by a misty street, black and wet, and harrowing cries that seemed one moment a man's, the next a beast's. He was not given to getting up in the night but he dressed and went outside to walk off the dreariness he'd woke to. A cold and brilliant moon brightened the ground fog which layered the pasture like a fallen cloud. The high ridge of hill behind his fields was ragged with wormshot spruce, wicks of branch against the sky. As a boy he'd walked those high woods with his grandfather who offered him the Gaelic names of things, most of them forgotten now, gone with the good trees. One day he'd told Bilkie about the words for heaven and hell, how they, Druid words, went far back before the time of Christ. *Ifrinn,* the Isle of the Cold Clime, was a dark and frigid region of venomous reptiles and savage wolves. There the wicked were doomed to wander, chilled to their very bones and bereft even of the company of their fellow sinners. And the old heaven, though the Christians kept that name too, was also different: *Flathinnis,* the Isle of the Brave, a paradise full of light which lay far distant, somewhere in the Western Ocean. "I like that some better," his grandfather had said. "Just the going there would be good. As for hell, nothing's worse than cold and loneliness."

As he moved through the fog, it thinned like steam, but gathered again and closed in behind him. Suddenly he heard hoofbeats. Faintly at first, then louder. He turned in a circle, listening. Not a cow of his. They were well-fenced. Maybe the Dunlop's next door. But cow or horse it was coming toward him at a good clip and yet he couldn't make it out, strain as he might. Soon his heart picked up the quick, even thud of the hooves, and when in the pale fog a shape grew and darkened and then burst forth, a head shaggy as seaweed and cruelly horned, he raised his arms wildly in a shout of fear and confusion as the bull shied past him, a dark rush of heat and breath, staggering him like a blow. Aw, that goddamn Highland bull, that ugly bugger. Trembling with anger and surprise, he listened to it crash through thickets off up the hill, the fog eddying in its wake, until Bella called him and he turned back to the house.

On the porch of the manse Bilkie waited for Mrs. MacQueen to answer the door. The porch Rev. Mac-Lean had built, but the white paint and black trim were Bilkie's work, donated last summer when his lobstering was done. He'd enjoyed those few days around the minister. One afternoon when Bilkie was on the ladder he thought he heard Gordon talking to himself, but no, he was looking up, shading his eyes. "It's only a mile from Mull, Iona," Gordon said to him. "Just across the Sound. So it's part of going home, really." Bilkie had said yes, he could see that. But he wasn't sure, even now, that he and the minister meant home in the same way. "Monks lived there, Bilkie. For a long, long time. They had a different view of the world, a different feel for it altogether. God was still *new* there, you see. Their faith was . . . robust."

Mrs. MacQueen, the housekeeper, filled the doorway and Bilkie told her what he would like.

"A book about Iona?" She was looking him up and down. She smelled of Joy, lemon-scented, the same stuff he used on his decks. "I don't read the man's books, dear, I dust them."

"He wouldn't mind me looking. Me and himself are friends." He rapped the trim of the door. "My paint."

"Well, he could have used some friends in Oban."

Mrs. MacQueen showed him into the minister's study, making it clear she would not leave. She turned the television on low, as if this were a sickroom, and sat down on a hassock, craning her ear to the screen.

Wine-colored drapes, half-drawn, gave the room a warm light. Bookshelves lined one wall, floor to ceiling, and Bilkie touched their bindings as he passed. He hadn't a clue where to begin or how to search in this hush: he only wanted to know more about that place, and maybe when the man returned they could talk about what went wrong there. But he felt shy with Mrs. MacQueen in the room. A map of Scotland was thumb-tacked to the wall. The old clan territories were done in bright colors. Lewis he spotted easily, and Mull. And tiny Iona. On the desktop, under sprigs of lilac in a small vase, he saw a slim red book. In it were notes in Gordon's hand. With a quick glance at the housekeeper, he took it to the leather chair close by the north window, a good bright spot where Gordon must have sat many a time, binoculars propped on the sill. Bilkie put them to his eyes instinctively. Behind the manse a long meadow ran down to the shore. Across the half mile of water his boat rocked gently in the light swells. Strange to see his yellow slicker hanging by the wheel, emptied of him. Moving the glasses slightly he made out Angus standing over his boy, Johnny hunched down into some work or other. Good with engines, was Johnny. Suddenly Angus looked toward Bilkie. Of course his eyes would take in only the white manse on the hill, and the church beside it. Yet Bilkie felt seen in a peculiar way and he put down the binoculars.

Aware of the time, he turned pages, reading what he could grasp. That Iona's founder, St. Columba, had sailed there from Ireland to serve his kinsmen, the Scots of Dalriada. That he and his monks labored with their own hands, tilling and building, and that in their tiny boats they spread the faith into the remote and lesser isles, converting even the heathen Picts. That even before he was born, Columba's glory had been foretold to his mother in a dream: "An angel of the Lord appeared to her, and brought her a beautiful robe—a robe which had all the colors of all the flowers of the world. Immediately it was rapt away from her, and she saw it spread across the heavens, stretched out over plains and woods and mountains. . . ." He read testaments to St. Columba's powers and example, how once in a great storm his ship met swelling waves that rose like mountains, but at his prayer they were stilled. He was a poet and loved singing, and songs praising Columba could keep you from harm. His bed was bare rock and his pillow a stone. During the three days and three nights of his funeral, a great wind blew, without rain, and no boat could reach or leave the island.

Bilkie was deep in the book when Mrs. Mac-Queen, exclaiming, "That's desperate, just desperate!", turned off the soap opera and came over to him.

"You'll have to go now," she said. "This isn't the public library, dear, and I have cleaning to do."

He would never talk himself past her again, not with Gordon away. He returned the book to the desk and followed her to the front door.

"Did you ever pray to a saint, Mrs. MacQueen?"

She crossed her arms. "I'm no R. C., Mr. Sutherland."

"I don't think that matters, Mrs. MacQueen. The minister has a terrible wound. Say a word to St. Columba."

"He's healing. He's getting better and soon might be coming home, is what I heard."

The next morning the sun glared up from a smooth sea as Bilkie hauled his traps, moving from one swing to another over the grounds his grandfather had claimed. By the time Bilkie was old enough to fish, there was a little money in it. But you had to work. Nobody ever gave it to you, and the season was short. He had started out young hauling by hand, setting out his swings in the old method, the backlines anchored with kellicks, and when he wasn't hauling he was rowing, and damned hard if a wind was on or the tide against you. He had always worked alone, rowed alone. Except when his boy was with him, and that seemed as brief now as a passing bird. He preferred it out here by himself, free of the land for awhile, the ocean at his back.

This season the water was so clear he could see ten fathoms, see the yellow backline snaking down, the traps rising. His grandfather told him about the waters of the West Indies, the clear blue seas with the sun so far down in them it wouldn't seem like drowning at all, for the light there.

He gaffed a buoy and passed the line over the hauler, drawing the trap up to the washboard where he quickly culled the dripping, scurrying collection. He measured the lobsters, threw a berried one back. But after he dropped the trap and moved on, he knew he'd forgotten, for the second time that morning, to put in fresh bait. To hell with it. On the bleak rocks of the Bird Islands shags spread their dark wings to dry. A school of mackerel shimmered near the boat, an expanding and contracting disturbance just beneath the surface as they fed. He cut the engine, letting the boat drift like his mind. He hummed the song of Johnny Carmichael but stopped. Couldn't get the damn tune out of his head. Sick of it. He picked a mackerel out of the bait box and turned it over in his hands, stroking the luminous flow of stripes a kind of sky was named for: a beautiful fish, if you looked at it—the smooth skin, dark yet silvery. Gordon MacLean said from the pulpit that a man should find beauty in what's around him, for that too was God. But for Bilkie everything had been so familiar, everything he knew and saw and felt, until Torquil died. He took out his knife and slid it slowly into the dead fish: now, what might that be like, a piece of steel like that inside you? A feeling you'd carry a long while, there, under the scar.

Astern, the head of the cape rose behind buff-colored cliffs, up into the deep green nap of the mountain. He had no fears here, never in weather like this when the sea was barely breathing. Still, he missed the man, the sound of his voice on Sunday. The last service before he left for Iona, the minister had read Psalm 44, the one, he said, that St. Columba sang to win the Picts away from their magi, the Druids . . . *O God, our fa-*

thers have told us, what work thou didst in their days, in the times of old. . . .

After Bilkie lost his son, he'd stayed away from church, from the mournful looks and explanations, why he should accept God's taking an innocent boy in such a way. His heart was sore, he told Bella, and had to heal up, and nothing in the church then could help it. But a few weeks after Rev. MacLean arrived, Bilkie went to hear him. Damn it, the man could preach. Not like those TV preachers who couldn't put out anything much but their palms and a phone number. A slender string it was that Gordon MacLean couldn't take a tune from. And only once had he mentioned Torquil in a roundabout way, to show he was aware there'd been a boy, that he knew what a son could mean.

As Bilkie turned in toward the wharf that afternoon, he saw three boats in ahead of him. Above Angus's blue and white Cape Islander the men had gathered in a close circle, talking and nodding. Only Johnny Carmichael was still down below, sitting on the gunnels with his guitar. Bilkie approached the wharf in a wide arc, trying to discern what he saw in the huddled men and the boy off alone bent into his instrument. He brought his boat up into the lee and flung a line to Angus who was waving for it.

"Bilkie, you're late, boy!" he shouted.

"Aw, I was feeling slow today!"

When the lines were secured, Angus called down to him. "Did you hear about it?"

"About what?"

"The minister, Bilkie, for God's sake! He's passed

away! It was sudden, you know. Complications. Not expected at all."

Bilkie's hands were pressed against a crate he'd been about to shift. He could feel the lobsters stirring under the wood. He looked up at Angus. "I knew that already," he said.

Instead of going home, Bilkie drove to a tavern fifteen miles away. He sat near a window at one of the many small tables. Complications. Lord. The sun felt warm on his hands and he watched bubbles rise in his glass of beer. The tavern was quiet but tonight it would be roaring. Peering into the dim interior he made out Jimmy Carey alone at a table. Jimmy was Irish and had acted cranky here more than once. But he seemed old and mild now, back there in the afternoon dark, not the hell-raiser he used to be. And wasn't St. Columba an Irishman, after all? Bilkie raised his glass and held it there until Jimmy, who looked as if he'd been hailed from across the world, noticed it and raised his own in return. Bilkie beckoned him over. They drank until well past supper, leaning over the little table and knocking glasses from time to time. Bilkie told him about St. Columba, about the monks in their frail vessels.

"You know about St. Brendan, of course," Jimmy said, his eyes fixing on Bilkie but looking nowhere. "They say he got as far as here even, and clear to Bermuda before he was done."

"Bermuda I know about." Bilkie tried to sing what he remembered. " 'Oh there be flowers in Bermuda, beauty lies on every hand . . . and there be laughter, ease and drink for every man. . . .' " He leaned close to Jimmy's face: " ' . . . but there not be joy for *me*.' "

On the highway Bilkie focused hard on the center line, thinking that Jimmy Carey might have bought one round at least, St. Brendan be damned. To the west the strait ran deep and dark, the sun just gone from it as he turned away toward home. Bad time to meet the mounties. He lurched to a stop by the roadside where a small waterfall lay hidden. He plunged through a line of alders into air immediately cool. The falls stepped gently through mossed granite, down to a wide, clear pool, and he remembered Bella bending her head into it years ago, her fair fanning out red there as she washed the salt away after swimming. He knelt and cupped the water, so cold he groaned, over his face again and again.

As he drove the curves the white church appeared and disappeared above the trees. When he came upon it, it seemed aloof, unattended. Cars were parked carelessly along the driveway to the manse, and Bilkie slowed down long enough to see a man and woman climbing the front steps, Mrs. MacQueen, in her flowered apron, waiting at the door. Oh, there'd be some coming and going today, the sharing of the hard news. When he felt the schoolhouse approaching, he vowed again not to look, not to bother what went on there. But he couldn't miss the blue tent in the front yard, and the life raft filled with water for a wading pool. This time he did not slow down. Too often he had wondered about the blow on the neck, about what his son had felt, and who, in that instant, he had blamed . . . something so simple as a window coming down on his bones. There. In a schoolhouse.

Bella had not seen Bilkie drunk like this in years, but she knew why and said nothing, not even about Rev. MacLean. She could not get him to come inside for supper. He reeled around angrily in the lower pasture, hieing cows away when they trotted toward the fence for handouts of fresh hay. He shouted up at the ridge. Finally he stalked to the back door.

"Gordon was going to Iona," he said to his wife. "He could check the fury of wild animals, that saint they had there. Did Gordon no damn good, eh?"

"You've had some drink, Bilkie, and I've had none. I'm tired now."

He stepped up close to her and took her face in his hands. "Ah, Bella. Your hair was so pretty."

She made him go to bed, but after dark he woke. He smelled of the boat and wanted to wash. Hearing a car, he went over to the window. Near his neighbor's upper pasture headlights bounced and staggered over the rough ground. They halted, backed up, then swept suddenly in another direction until the shaggy bull galloped across the beams. Loose again. A smallish, wild-looking beast they'd imported from Scotland. Could live out on its own in the dead of winter, that animal. You might see it way off in a clearing, quiet, shouldering snow like a monument. The headlights, off again in pursuit, captured the bull briefly but it careened away into the darkness, and the car—a Dunlop boy at the

wheel no doubt—raked the field blindly. Complications. A stone for a pillow. His own boy would be a
man now. Passed away, like a wave.

It was difficult for Bilkie to get up that day. He had
always opened his eyes on the dark side of four a. m.
but now Bella had to push and coax him. He sat on the
edge of the bed for a long time staring at the half-model
of a schooner mounted on the wall. His grandfather
had worked her, the *Ocean Rose,* lost on Hogsty Reef in
the Bahamas with his Uncle Bill aboard.

"You don't get up anymore. What's the matter with
you?" Bella said. He took the cup of coffee she held out
to him, nodding vaguely. Squalls had lashed the house
all night and now a thick drizzle whispered over the
roof. "You know Rev. MacLean is coming home this
day, and tonight they'll wake him."

"I can't go," Bilkie said.

"What would he think, you not there at his wake
with the others who loved him?"

"He's not thinking at all anymore. That's just a
body there, coming back."

"Don't be terrible. Don't be the way you were after
Torquil."

"They could have buried him over there. Couldn't
they have? Near where he wanted to go?"

"He was born *here,* Bilkie. Nobody asked, I don't
suppose, one way or the other."

He could see that she'd been crying. He put the
coffee down carefully on the window sill and took her
hands in his, still warm from the cup. "Bella, dear," he

61

said. "You washed your hair in that water. It must have hurt, eh? Water so cold as that?"

Gusts rocked the car as Bilkie crossed the bridge that joined the other island. He was determined to take himself out of the fuss, some of it from people who would never bestir themselves were Gordon MacLean here and breathing. Above him the weather moved fast. The sky would whiten in patches but all the while churn with clouds black as the cliffs by the lighthouse. There was a good lop on the water, looking east from the bridge, and when the strait opened out a few miles away the Atlantic flashed white against an ebbing tide.

In the lee of the wharf the lobster boats were surging like tethered horses. No one was around. The waves broke among the pilings beneath him and the timbers creaked. He walked to the seaward end where Angus had stacked his broken traps. Across the roughening water the manse looked small, the cars tiny around it. Every morning his grandfather would say, old as he was, *Dh'iarr am muir a thadhal.* The sea wants to be visited.

He threw off his lines and headed out into the strait, rounding up into the wind, battering the waves until he checked back on the throttle. In the turns of wind he smelled the mackerel in the bait box, the fumes of the engine. But as he drew abreast of Campbell Point, a gust of fragrance came off the land and he strained to see its source in the long, blowing grass of the point. It was quickly gone and there was nothing to account for it but what had been there all along—the thin line of beach, the grass thick as hay all the way back to the woods. To the west, on the New Skye Road, he glimpsed St. David's Church, a small white building behind a veil of rain, set in the dense spruce, no one there now but Bible Camp kids in the summer.

The sea was lively at the mouth of the strait where wind and tide met head to head. He bucked into the whitecaps, slashes of spray cracking over the bow. The waves deepened as the sea widened out but he'd ride better when he reached the deeper water where the breaking crests would cease. He had a notion of the West Indies, of his grandfather under sails, out there over the curve of the world and rolling along in worse weather than this. Hadn't the Irish monks set out in their currachs of wickerwork and hide, just for the love of God? They had survived. They reached those islands they sailed for, only dimly sure where they were. But maybe you could come by miracles easier then, when all of life was harder, and God closer to the sea than he was now. Now with no saints around, saints who could sow a field and sail a boat, you had to find your own miracles. You couldn't travel to them, could you, Gordon, boy?

He would have to go back. He would have to stand at the wake holding his hat like the rest of them, looking at Gordon who'd come dead such a distance. Bilkie watched the rhythm of the waves. He needed a break in them to bring his boat around and run with the sea. But then he wasn't hearing the engine anymore, and the boat was falling away, coming around slowly with no more sound than a sail would make. Columba. A dove. Strange name for a man. *Colmcille. Caoir gheal,* his grandfather called waves like these. A bright flaming of white. The sea had turned darker than the sky, and over the land the boat was swinging toward, clouds lay heavy and thick, eased along like stones, dark as dolmens. "Ah!" was all Bilkie said when the wave rose under him, lifting the boat high like an offering.

WORK

As Jack MacBain was struggling once again to get beyond the first few bars of "Devil in the Kitchen," Little Norman wanted to tell him the dream. He had dreamed of the quarry again last night—the high white gypsum cliff trembling with heat, and under its blazing face hunks of white rock that Jack and him had split. But now Jack was driving his fiddle hard and close to the floor, as he had earlier that evening down at the Fire Hall where dancers, to that deep Cape Breton stroke, beat the floorboards like the skin of a drum. Then Jack had faltered—not that the dancers cared so long as he caught it up again—but he'd slowed up and slowed up and then lost it, lost the tune like you'd step in a hole, his ruddy face redder and his eyes bright with embarrassment. In mid-stroke he'd had to quit, just as he was quitting now.

"No use to this," Jack said. He stared down at the fiddle on his lap and scratched the bow along the side of his neck as if this might draw the tune from his memory. "Jesus, boy. I think I'm done out."

"And you, Norman," Jack's wife called from the corner where her anger had placed her. "You had to encourage him, eh? Not for a minute was he fit to play a dance, everyone looking on."

"I *was* fit," Jack said hotly. "You got to play for dances. Dancers *make* you play, make you good." He lay the fiddle and bow on the kitchen table beside the open lid of the case. "All I needed was a little rum. And you didn't give me any."

"Sure, Dalena," Norman said, feeling miserable enough without the blame. "It was a farewell, like, and maybe just a splash . . ."

"Some farewell, that," Dalena said. She frowned. "He don't need to be remembered that way, the tunes leaving him." She sat on a box and hugged herself, surrounded by the belongings they would take to the Senior Citizens Home in the morning. Norman looked at her hands: girl's hands they were, even yet. And her hair still mostly black when it had every reason to be white. She it was, small and busy, had waited on Jack when he was home, put him to bed when he was drunk and roaring. But the rest of the time when he was away it had been Norman who'd seen to him, wherever they worked—mines, mill, lumberwoods. The quarry too.

"We'll remember how he *played,* Dal," Norman said, hurt, "not how he quit." Shame enough to see a big man go back, and a fine fiddler to boot. Lungs choking up, kidneys half-shot. But the *mind*—that struck him hard, poor Jack, not knowing the tunes anymore, a man who, many a time, had driven his fiddle down right to the last dancer reeling at sunrise.

"Take it, Norman," Jack said. "Take it with you home tonight, that fiddle. I'm done."

"Aw, I'm no fiddler. Come on, boy, don't be so glum."

"Dal?" Jack said gravely. "For sure I'm needing a little rum." He stared at the floor and let a few deep breaths rattle in his lungs for pity. But Dalena was running her bifocals along a row of small plastic bottles on the window sill.

"You know what Dr. Fraser told you," she said, stern as a nurse. "Time for your medicine anyway."

"A little celebration," Jack said. "Look at it like that, girl, not like Dr. Fraser."

"And what are we celebrating then?" she said, her back to them.

"Don't be so hard, Dal," Little Norman said. "You two off and away in the morning, and me back up the road without a soul."

"Rum won't change any of that, Norman. And you've got your health and no worries. Like you say, a fiddler you're not."

Norman had his scars, sure, and pains now and then to go with them. And some days his blood seemed to go slack like he'd just done two shifts in a mine. A bit of sleep cured that. And hard work. Work could make him forget most anything—a damn good knack to have, so his dad once told him. As for his eye blinded in the pit, it was like coming on a corner he could never quite turn and sometimes he had to cock his head like a rooster. But these were not worries, true, not worries the way Dalena meant. Anyway, it wasn't her sympathy he was after tonight: he just wished she were feeling more easy. Goodbyes were hard enough.

Jack had seized the fiddle and bow again and was cutting into "The Black Sporran," but it soon tapered off into a groping whine. He whacked the instrument back onto the table.

"Give us a drink, Dal," he said. "For the love of Jesus." He was breathing in a kind of growl but without much steam behind it.

"Your cuts are sharp as ever, Jack," Little Norman said quietly.

"Aw, frig, might as well give that bow back to the fairies where it came from."

"Jack," Dalena said, counting the pills in her palm. "There's lemonade in the icebox."

There was a time when Norman would have seen his pal, with the back of that big hand, sweep those pills to the floor. Not now. Dal didn't fear his storms anymore. She was seeing to him now, up one side and down the other, just like Little Norman had through sixty-odd years of work, not only in the lumberwoods but in the steel mill too when they shared rooms in Sydney and had one hell of a time out on the town, racketing about.

"I don't want pills," Jack said. "And I don't want iced piss either. I'll buy my *own* rum when we get to that goddamn home. I'll get a taxi."

Dalena would have ducked and whispered in the old days but now she held the pills tight and stood in his face.

"There's a new chapter in your life tomorrow, Jack," she said. "And there's no rum in it."

"Last frigging chapter, then. You can shut the damn book too. Norman, tell this woman about rum. Tell her what it *means,* boy."

"I know what it means," Dalena said.

Norman slid to the edge of his chair. He cleared his throat. "You talk about sick? Jack and me, well now, we *worked* our way through sick spells, for Jesus sake, our eyes so hot with fever they'd glow in the dark. It was all the medicine we had, eh? A good slug of Demerrara? Now that was rum, by God."

Jack smiled. "You could dip it with a spoon. Like molasses. Smooth as a kiss, that."

"Drink it all night and no harm the next morning. Roll out like a baby. Rumrunning days, best rum in the world. Triple X Black Diamond, and a right jewel it was."

Flushed with the memory, Jack picked up the bow like a stick from the ground and tapped it on his knee, leaving a faint mark like chalk.

"We rummed up a lot that summer of the steel strike."

"'22 was it? '23?"

"Bloody Sunday I'm taking about. We broke the Sabbath good with the bottle Rod MacLeod gave us. But we didn't scamper, did we? You get good Black Diamond under your belt, the provincial police can go hang, and everything else." He looked darkly at Dalena.

"Terrible work anyway, that mill. Fires in your face. Rather break rock," Little Norman said.

"Sure, cut wood. Out in the air, good air. Give us a sharp crosscut and we'd do seven cord a day, eh, Norman? And what cut the cold? *Rum*. Not too much, now, no. Just a snapper."

"And no goddamn provincials there, boy. But you was never scared of them, Jack. Didn't care who it was or where the hell or what."

"They cracked you good too, Norman, chased you down."

"Oh, Jesus, them hardwood batons." Little Norman fingered a hard ridge of flesh that parted his spiky hair. "Skullbusters." But it was a horse he remembered most. Coalhaulers' horses they were, nags, most of them, mounts commandeered by the provincial police who'd somehow suffocated fourteen of their own en route from Halifax to Sydney in a box car. Drunk, the whole gang of them, charging churchgoers, anybody— striker or not—on the sidewalk that fine June evening. Norman had felt the horse behind him, its breath and its bulk, heard the creak and strain of leather. And when he turned around, it was to see that horse's eye rolling white and dirty, and the horse's bared, worn teeth champing, and then higher up a four-foot baton was already descending through a dangerous whiff of rum that was not his own. The wood opened up his head like you'd put a razor to it. But he'd never forgot the look in that horse's eye—some kind of old torment that Little Norman instantly understood.

"Policemen? Drunken bastards!" Jack said, stroking his thighs so rapidly the provincials might have been on the road outside. "Bloody Sunday, boy!" He glared at his fiddle as though he would smash it.

Dalena said nothing. When they went on like this she ignored them, like an old soldier's wife who'd too often heard battle songs she never had the urge to sing.

"And what did we get from that strike anyway?" Jack went on.

"A few frigging pennies," Norman answered, "nothing more. A bit of free coal."

"God, we needed that rum to stay *alive*. Dal doesn't know."

"I know more than you think," Dalena said wearily. She held out a tumbler of water which Jack ignored, looking around her at his chum.

"Try the lumberwoods in winter without rum," he said, louder. "Smash a finger or a toe and no doctor at all!"

Norman smiled. Sounding like the old Jack, he was. How many days had Norman roused him out of his bunk, those mornings in the lumberwoods, cold and dark, coaxing him to the cookroom where a big breakfast finally got him out of the dumps? The rest of the day they could outwork any men, big or little, even if it took some rum on the side. But there in the Senior Citizens Home, how would Dalena get the man moving?

How would she raise his spirits on a dreary winter morning, no work and no rum ahead of him?

"What difference would a taste of it make?" Jack shouted. His huge head, nearly bald now, was damp with sweat. "Well, I'll tell you," he answered, more evenly. "Life and death!"

"Don't get heated up, Jack," Dalena said. "There's none of it in the house anyway. But this you have to take. Now open."

Jack accepted the pills on his tongue like poison and took a mouthful of water, scowling. "Dr. Yango'd let me have rum."

Dalena glanced out the window at the cottage next door. A Filipino doctor from Sydney Mines had built it for summers and brought his family down on weekends.

"He'd never," she said. "Don't kid yourself."

"They were at the dance, and having a good time too," Little Norman said. He wished Dalena would have a good time, or go tend to something like she used to and leave him and Jack alone. They hadn't a chance to talk much this night, not like they did with just the two of them. On the Yangos' front porch facing the water hung a cylinder of vivid, humming blue. Norman knew she liked the doctor, an important man, in a way she could never like him.

"Strange, that bug light," he said. "Singes flies like hair in a candle, but the flies are all gone."

"Well, it's a comfort to me when the Doctor is down, I can tell you," Dalena said. "If Jack was to have a turn, I'd only need shout and . . ."

"Norman!" Jack yelled, his hands on his ears. "Got anything on your hip?"

"I do, Jack. Good stuff, too."

Dalena turned her furious eyes on Norman. "And *you* his friend?"

"Aw, Dal, the man needs a lift. Just a taste wouldn't hurt, the size of him."

"Size got nothing to do with it, Norman. He's sick."

Jack was looking down at his hands, opening and closing them slowly as if he wanted to grab something. "I'll get a taxi," he mumbled, "when we're there. You wait."

Dalena shivered and rubbed her arms. "We need a fire in that stove, then I'll make tea. Could you fetch some wood, Norman?

"What, am I crippled?" Jack said, rising. "Can't split wood? God almighty, I'm man enough for that. Let's go, Norman, give me a hand, boy."

"Now wait. . . ." Dalena appealed to Norman, but he gave her a solemn nod and she relented.

Jack eased himself down the back steps and shambled to the woodpile, Norman just behind him, glad to be free of Dalena. Under the faint light from the kitchen window Jack waited with the axe while Norman set up a short log on the chopping block.

"Might as well do this with the fiddle," Jack said as he split the log clean. "She'd burn nice."

"No, Jack, no. You'll get the tunes again, boy."

"A time comes, Norman, when the well she don't fill up no more. Maybe I got to go on a machine pretty soon." He raised the axe high above his head and brought it down with such force the halved wood flew. "A goddamn machine."

Norman did not want the details. He glanced up at the pill bottles silhouetted in the window, then reached down for another log and set it up, watching Jack bring the axe down with a grunt. The dull crack of the wood sounded fine to Norman, the power of it.

"Not like that fourteen pound sledgehammer, Jack," he said.

"Eh?"

"Ten cents more a day they paid you at the quarry. You could swing that goddamn big sledge, Jack. You were a breaker, boy."

"Was I now?" He sank the axe head hard into the block and stood back, his breath shooting into the cold air of an east wind. Leaves hustled in eddies around their feet, and through spruce trees across the road the surface of the strait shivered with light from the opposite shore. Norman liked it here by the water. He himself lived back up in the rear near the old mine where the mountain levelled out and trees shut you away from the sea. Boston people owned the place and kept him on there to look out for it. They only came for a month in the summer and he was glad when they left. All he'd needed since a long time was a room and a bed, and Jack down the road.

"God," Jack whispered hoarsely. "Give us a taste, Norman. What the hell, eh? Quick now or she'll be at the door."

Norman worked the pint of rum out of his back pocket and drank, sighing with a satisfaction deeper than the rum itself. Then he put it in Jack's hand like a corpsman. "This is the medicine. Take it slow, let it work awhile, boy." He rubbed his hands together and the heat of his palms brought back the first time they'd shared a bottle, yowling their way home through the woods.

"Kind of rips at me now." Jack shuddered. "Had none for weeks." He took another long draw. "You know, Norman, I swear the fairies were up in the trees there one night. Lord Jesus, they were pale too, white like." He stared at the dark spruce that ran thickly up the mountainside. "They want my bow back. They know I'm done with it, you see."

"Aw, the fairies are gone, gone, Jack. Don't get started on that."

"You think I'm foolish."

"Pass the bottle, boy. Let's go on a tear."

They exchanged the pint quietly like conspiritors. Norman settled down on the woodpile, his head pleasantly warm.

"Jack? You recall that quarry we worked in a while? Just lads then."

Jack pulled the axe out and sat down on the chopping block. He held the rum with both hands, staring down at it. "Eh?"

"It was long ago, Jack, long ago. We was walking high up over the face one evening, just about dark. The railroad tracks fanned out down below there, all shined up. Like silver, in that last light of the day going. Now there's something, you said. Beauty there, says Jack, and I says, yes, boy, there is. We stood up there watching till dark."

"Drinking too?" said Jack dully. He was checking the rum in the bottle against the light of the kitchen. He upended it and drank.

"No, no, not the night I'm talking about. . . . Strange, you know. I've had this dream about the quarry. Sometimes it's day and the heat's fierce. Then night, and the cliffs all lit up with them carbide flares. Damn it, but there's a pile of rock behind us and all around everywhere. And I can hear your sledge going, and them lights hissing the way they did. We'd been breaking stone in that place since day one, it seemed like. Just a dream, you know."

But Jack was swaying back and forth and humming with a strong beat, something that sounded like "Farewell to Whisky," Jack clogging heavily with one foot, stamping it down again and again. And then he stopped. He drank at the rum so long that Norman, with an eye toward the kitchen, carefully pulled it away. "Easy, boy. Let's rest a spell." But without wiping it he hastened the bottle to his own lips and took a swallow that set him coughing. Next door the bug lamp was extinguished but he could still see a faint bluish afterlight where it had hung and that bothered him. "Jack, you remember up Marble Mountain, that quarry there. . . .?"

"Bloody *Sunday*!" Jack roared, and there was Dalena's shadow at the door and she calling them. Just for a moment Norman hated her, the suddenness of her voice.

Jack, protesting, wavered to his feet and started for the house in a determined stagger. Christ, the man was half-cut already! Norman rushed after him grabbing for his arm as he climbed the back steps like rungs on a ladder, but Jack yanked it away and pushed into the kitchen, blurting bits of melody he'd ripped from one tune or another, Norman feeling hot from the rum but a little fearful when he saw Dalena rolling her eyes in disgust. Aw, girl, give us a grin. "Back from the lumber-woods, are you?" she said. Jack was whirling around like a bear, his rags of song getting smaller and smaller until they were no more than sounds, rising and falling. Dizzied, he fell into a chair and Dalena bent to look at his face. "Jesus, Norman," she said. "What were you drinking out there, gasoline?" Dal never said things like "Jesus."

"Just a little Captain Morgan, and not much of it either. He's after getting sensitive to it, I guess, eh?"

She looked at him in wonderment. "How can you be so old, Norman, and still so dumb? Help me get him to bed."

Jack did not resist, slumping his arms around them as they guided him into the bedroom and sat him on the edge of the mattress. Norman had never seen him like this, never in the longest or hardest work they'd done. He reached down to unlace his pal's shoes but Dalena took his arm and walked him to the doorway. "Listen, Norman, dear," she said gently, still holding his arm.

"You had the best of his life. Did you know that? You, not me. Now leave him like he is. I'll tend to him."

Norman stepped back from her, troubled by her sudden tenderness. He had rather she'd slapped him, harped at him, and he didn't know why. He looked desperately at Jack, but the man was lost in a mutter of rum.

"He'll want the fiddle again, Dal," Norman said, almost in a whisper. "He'll be wanting that."

"No. Take it. Maybe that's finished now. Can't you see?"

"He just gets in those moods, you know, and. . . ." Dalena smiled but she was not listening. "Aw, well . . . you'll need a fire, girl. I'll get the wood in."

But when he returned with an armload of kindling she was gone into the bedroom. He listened to her through the closed door weaving her voice softly around her husband. She would be taking off his shoes, helping him out of his big wool shirt. Norman set the wood by the stove. He looked again at the bedroom door.

"See you in the morning, eh, Jack?" he called out, as he had so many times in the past, though never had he posed it like a question. Hearing no answer, he left, the fiddle case tucked under his arm like a lunchpail.

Children's voices, pitched high with excitement, drifted out an open window of the doctor's cottage. Little Norman thought it might be nice to stop in, but he went on down the road, walking in the middle until a car honked him over to the shoulder. He did not wave, knowing they were strangers. Strangers outnumbered the old families now in New Skye. "Great for leaving, these Cape Bretoners," his dad used to say when someone he liked had picked up and gone. And there was Jack leaving at last, and laying his fiddle down too. Seemed you laid this thing down and that, and then yourself. After that, God took care of it, so they said. But it troubled him to think of Jack. He'd heard about people who faded fast once they went off to the Home. Looked forward to it, others had said, what with the new building and the new apartments right downtown where you were handy to everything. But that wasn't the whole story—games and singsongs and store windows up the street. That's what Dalena spoke of, but then she'd never had much, poor girl, growing up around the quarry where the sky above was all you saw of the world.

Weary, Norman squatted on a stone by the roadside. At his feet the bank dropped sharply to the shore of the strait. Across the water a wharf light flickered in the currents. He uncapped the rum: a sharp and sweet but lonely taste it was, just medicine. Oh God, he'd like to go on a good bat. But not alone. It's friends you want when you're flushed and gabby. He reached out to touch the cold bark of a birch tree. Winter there, and in the smell of leaves too, darkening underfoot. Soon would come that raw turn of wind, that first fiery breath in your throat that made you think of ice. They had come close to death once, him and Jack together, their last time over in the Black Country. Norman had never cared for the mines, deep in the dark. But work was precious. Sometimes he thought he could still smell it, the firedamp. No, they said, there's no odor, but oh, a word he could taste, that stink of methane or whatever it was, a bog smell. Flaring their noses in that air thick with sweat and water, they had stopped their picks in mid-swing and fixed their lamps on each other's look, Jack's eyes white as a minstrel's. Somewhere down the disappearing shaft bad air found a bit of flame. Thunder and dust then, roaring over them like a nightmare train. When he woke, there was sunlight all over the room, sun in the window. He thought he was dead, and Jack along with him. But above him a doctor said, "You're tough as a rat."

When Little Norman woke, for a moment he might've been twenty again and the quarry out there waiting for the bend of his back. But in the open closet a circle of sunlight had penetrated the gloom of his clothes. The light told him first that he had missed them, that by now they would be on their way, and then it told him he would miss them like hell.

He dressed slow as a child. Never did he sleep so late into the day, and wouldn't it have to be this one. The fiddle case lay open on the chest of drawers. He plinked the strings but their sound was only painful. Where was the bow? He knelt under bed and bureau, patted the dark: it was nowhere in the room. He swayed a little when he stood. By God, Jack, he thought, where are we, after all? He pressed his fingers along the wood of the fiddle: he could feel the music that had been there, and he wouldn't need the bow.

In the kitchen he stood with a mug of black coffee, cupping its warmth. Was that a sparkle of frost on the window? Outside the wind was stripping down the woods, driving whirls of leaves across the field. Why had so much failed out? Only a handful of farms left now. The coal mine, pulp mills, quarries. Desperate small wages, but work. Something should have stuck here, something they'd toiled over. No, you were left staring at your hands and that was the end of it. No work today, boy. Nothing to cut down or bust up, to shovel or haul or drag. You didn't have to be a Giant MacAskill who could hoist a ton on his back. We got our tons right enough, boy. How many did we move? Put that in our timebook. Cut it in a gravestone. Find some of that good marble on Marble Mountain and put up a rough stone for me and Jack, for all of us who traipsed these mountains looking for work like sheep looking for grass. Was there a man now who would shovel snow day and night, drifts as deep as a barn and the wind playing the devil? Like the world was an hour-glass and you digging there in the bottom of it. There was no more men like them and no more to come like them. Aw, goddamn it, he didn't want to be bitter.

In the woodshed where old tools were stored he located the sledgehammer under scraps of lumber. The shaft was grey, its grain coarsened, the head rusty. But she was still tight, couldn't fly off if you swung her. He gripped the handle: Jesus, there'd been times in his life when he thought just his own strength could bring him something better, often on mornings like this, urged by that fear of winter, a touch of frost giving way maybe for the last time to heat of the sun. Can I outwit you, boy? Can I buy your mill or your mine? No, by God, I can't. But I can outwork you to hell and back again.

He set off down the New Skye Road, the sledge on his shoulder. Coming on Jack's house his heart quickened hoping maybe they'd been delayed. But no one answered his knock and he walked around outside like a burglar twisting doorknobs and hooding his eyes at the windows. Gone. Every box and barrel.

It was a long walk to the highway. The sun slid in and out of the morning, warming him, then leaving him to shiver in the cold gusts off the strait. The shaft of the hammer chafed him and he welcomed the rest when he put his thumb to cars gathering speed for the mountain. He waited in their backwash until a plumber's van pulled over. The young man behind the wheel grinned at the sledge but said sure, he was going that way and would leave Little Norman where he wanted. They traded ready lines about the weather but talked no further. A transistor radio lay on the seat and blared into the space between them. "Here would suit me fine," Norman said when they neared the stretch he remembered.

After he left the road and stepped into the trees he was lost. The old railroad should have been somewhere about but the newer spruce had established themselves among older birch and maple and beech whose last leaves hung sparse and papery in the wind. He wandered randomly until the sun broke free again and he could get his bearings. When he found the old railbed he kept to it despite the alders and tough, stunted spruce trying to obliterate it as they did any land a man left to them. And before long he recognized the rubble that had been dumped and spread, and sometimes it looked like a land not part of this place at all but somewhere else in the world where stone, weathered grey and fine, was the earth you planted in, where hardy trees took hold, their roots like panicked fingers in the soil. The narrow gauge rails were gone, spikes, ties, the works, taken up for scrap. But he could follow the turnings, even with the trees high up beside him, crowding, lashing his face when he was too tired to fend them off. The grade was a long, slow climb. He caught the sulphur smell of a spring, glimpsed the red stems of dogwood concealing it. His bad eye beat hard and he was thirsty. Too early for water. Not even noon yet, and he'd have to earn that first sweet cupful. Finally the bed levelled off toward the quarry. He could see the ragged cliffs and chimneys sculpted into shapes he could not recall, honeycombed by rains and run-off, the white rock creased with red bleeding down from the clay above. He had forgotten how high they ran, how deeply he had been here working among the ruck. Hummocks of scrub grass and tufts of weeds spread across the floor of the quarry. Rough heaps lay half-split and spilled like the day the last man left, though for a time kids from the valley, cousins of Dalena, had hurled their share of stones here, tussled for king of the mountain. But now the sun was weak. The faces of the cliffs were cool and darkened like old ice. From high on a rim between broken trees a deer gazed down at him. He imagined its

POPLARS

As Neil approached the rest home and saw the old men in wheelchairs like plants put out to sun, he remembered his uncle running—even as a man he had run for the hell of it, his long legs pounding through pasture grass, scattering cows in all directions. But now Neil spotted Lauchie among the patients by the doorway and was relieved he would not have to run that gauntlet of infirmity to his uncle's room, an ordeal that left him dark for hours afterward. He waved, and Lauchie, as if to distinguish himself from the tilted and pillowed men around him, worked his chair forward, first one wheel, then the other, tacking his way. The hand he held out as Neil reached him trembled with strain, but his grip had the old strength in it.

"The hay, Neilie, is it ripening?"

"Into the first bloom, the last I saw, Lauchie."

"Time to cut." He shook his head. "Past time, even."

His uncle looked broad and sturdy in the chair, and there was no mistaking the sports coat of Cape Breton tartan, that bold flag of his spirits. The nurses had trimmed his thick mustache, whose peppery gray only suggested its former blackness, and his curly hair, white now that had been so black like his brows, they had called him The Crow.

The sun was hot in the pavement and made no easier the struggle to pull him across the varnished board and into the car. But Neil could handle his uncle's weight now without heaving him around like stone. Lauchie hated this helplessness, his face flaring with shame by the time Neil had him straight in the seat. He stared ahead, his jaws tight, until they were free of the home. "*Beannachd-leat,*" he said. Farewell.

For a long while after his stroke Lauchie had refused to talk. His mushy words had embarrassed him even more than his useless right arm and legs. But Neil, home on a rare visit from California, was determined that his uncle not fade into silence. He visited him frequently, looked in on his farm every week or two, and reported back, as if his uncle's return to it were a certainty. He had talked at Lauchie at first, not with him, but soon memories that had lain dormant for years came slowly to life. Lauchie began to join in with details, bits and pieces. By midsummer he had moved from a code of phrases and words, for which Neil provided a framework, to whole sentences. It was a new language Lauchie uttered slowly and carefully, as if the words were bubbles about to burst before their shapes were seen.

They took the old highway out of town, along the arm of the bay sheltered behind the slopes of Beinn Bhreagh. Banks of lupine were still blooming. On long slow wings a blue heron rose out of a marsh of cattails and sedge. Lauchie seemed absorbed in the sights he'd been deprived of since they found him unconscious by his mailbox four months back. A chestnut horse grazed by the roadside fence; children foraged along the shoulder for berries. But he scowled at a mobile home recently dropped in the middle of a meadow.

"They're not houses at all."

"Houses are expensive, Lauchie."

"A piece of land like that, you don't want a trailer. You want wood, stone. Something to last."

Something to last, yes. All summer in his mother's house Neil had struggled against a twilight over which he had no control. He had always said he would come back here—refusing to use the word "retire," which meant something quite different—but without having to consider what that might mean, then or later. Now it seemed that the land as he'd known it was passing away, and some deep part of him was passing with it. He felt a distance growing between him and this place, not in miles but years. On his last journey to Cape Breton, a rushed plane flight to his father's death a decade ago, his relatives had seemed ageless, forever in a state of elderly good health. Now many were gone or fading badly, their land in limbo or under strange names. All conversations came round to illness, to death, and the churchyard he could see from his bedroom had three new stones since the first of June. His mother had sold all but a few acres of their place, and weekend cottages had popped up along the shore. Neil had arrived to stay a month—his long-awaited retreat from a crowded California town, from teaching school, yes, even from his own wife and children to whom Cape Breton was a dim and distant place. Instead he had stayed on, hoping to see Lauchie reclaim his farm and somehow hold it. But the last time Neil visited the farm he had pulled up the driveway only a short distance and sat there, the motor running, as he watched the house, the fields. Nothing had moved but the hay, slow and stiff with the burden of rain. The place seemed suspended, waiting, and Neil had eased off the brake, backing slowly down to the road.

Curving into the TransCanada, Neil picked up speed toward Kelly's Mountain. For the most part the highway followed the route of the old road with short pieces of it left off to the side here and there like small abandoned airstrips.

"I remember when rains killed the traffic dead on this road," his uncle said, angling the wing window for a breeze. "You went by boat or you didn't go."

"Oars or a little sail, eh?"

"Was fine on a fair day, on some worse than mud. You were keen on boats, Neilie. That I remember."

From South Haven they headed up the steepening

grade of the mountain. St. Ann's Bay grew more beautiful below them as they climbed. Lauchie beckoned to the look-off and Neil pulled into it and shut off the engine. The ticking of its metal was the only sound apart from an occasional car shooting past behind them. Neil had hoped only for sun today. Their other outings had been soured with rain or dark skies, no help to either of them, Lauchie glum and quiet in his baggy cardigan because the doctor wouldn't let him go all the way to the farm. Now they watched a lone lobster boat cut a line across the broad, deeply blue water below, its white hull picking up the white speck of lighthouse on MacLeod's Point. A station wagon with Connecticut plates drew in beside them and its family spilled out. Lauchie watched two small boys walk the guardrail like a tightrope. He smiled, having a weakness for kids, and much of his running had been for their amusement. But one of the boys caught sight of the famous tartan coat and pointed rudely, grinning toward his brother. Lauchie, who once would have twirled and said, "Some cloth, eh boys?" turned away, and Neil started the car.

On the south side of the mountain they swung onto the dirt road to New Skye. Rains had gouged the potholes deeper, and Neil threaded his way around them on the single narrow lane following the seaward foot of the mountain. The Bras d'Eau was visible through a line of birch and ratty spruce hanging on with the last of their roots. Then the trees ended and the road dropped level with a thin strip of rocky shore.

"Ho, Neilie, there's Angus!" Lauchie said. A few

feet from the shoulder the water fell off deep and Angus Chisholm, a cousin, set traps there. He was idling his boat intently toward a yellow buoy marker as Lauchie waved out the window. Neil blew the horn and Angus looked up, bracing himself in the bobbing boat and shading his eyes with no sign of recognition. He gaffed the buoy and slipped its line over the hauler, drawing the trap up from the bottom.

"I've changed," Lauchie said, lowering his hand. "I'm looking different now."

Neil wondered how his uncle had perceived these last months. Surely they had seemed indefinite and vague while he lay adrift in strange white rooms, crying out in Gaelic which no one attending him could understand. For the first time in seventy-seven years he had not slept and wakened under his own roof.

They were moving slowly enough for Neil to make out a family of sandpipers, the chicks darting over the rocks by the roadside as the mother veered toward the car to distract it. "Look there, Lauchie! *Luatharan-glas!*"

"Yes, yes . . . with young. Careful now."

He had taught Neil the Gaelic names of birds when he was a boy. Even now a sparrow in a city gutter was *gealan*. When older, Neil had browsed through his uncle's big Gaelic dictionary because he liked the sketches of flowers and fish, the parts of a boat, a plow. "So many of those words are going unspoken," Lauchie had said over his shoulder, "and words die, too, like anything that lives."

Neil eased around a boulder the mountain had disgorged onto this toehold road. The boulders seemed to grow more immense, great hunks of granite resting man-high on the narrow shore where the grader had shoved them. Neil saw a car coming up fast in the mirror.

"There he is," he muttered. "That damn kid from up the Cape." He watched the car rush up behind. Knowing the kid would kiss his bumper until he let him by, he hugged the shoulder and gritted his teeth as the car tore past, swaying and drumming over the ruts. Bits of gravel splattered the door like BBs, and a fine spray of mud layered the windshield.

"What's down there he's in such a hurry to?" Lauchie said.

"Mrs. MacKenzie's. Her nephew, Ma says, down for the summer. The little bastard will kill someone before he kills himself, I'm afraid." More than once Neil had encountered him on the road, dust billowing like a parachute behind him. He seemed to tear aimlessly in and out of New Skye, leaving a wake of fury.

They skirted the shore of the wide cove where boys were chucking stones at a pile of dead crabs dumped from a lobsterman's traps. Out on the listing wharf someone was bending into a dive—a dark figure with the sun bright behind him. Lauchie squinted for a glimpse of his boat. It was beached, uncalked and bottom up, beside a battered dory. Neil slowed, but his uncle only nodded at the flaking strakes. The boat was finished for him.

Beyond the cove they passed the ruins of a barn, a tangled heap of gray lumber receding into alder thickets and second-growth spruce, and soon Neil stopped at the mailbox with L. D. Chisholm lettered neatly on its side. He knew Lauchie would check it even though his mail was forwarded to the home. His uncle reached out the window awkwardly and lowered the door, staring into the box before gently shutting it. "Just spiders, Neilie." But he seemed unwilling to leave, his hand pressed against the door, his heavy brows closed in a frown, as if he were trying to remember what had happened here. When he had emerged from days of delirium, strapped to the bed because he had torn his oxygen tent to ribbons, he had told Neil's mother he wished he were dead. He had been struck down like a tree, he said, top to roots. Neil thought perhaps that's how it was now in his mind, a memory of lightning.

They hadn't climbed the driveway more than halfway up when the rain-slickened ruts and the incline sent the car lurching sideways, tires whining.

"Hell, I guess we slog it from here," Neil said.

His uncle sighed. It would be tough, with the slope and the damp grass. Neil sat gathering the will. Heat built up quickly in the car and he caught the faintest whiff from the bag of groceries in the back seat, the haddock and potatoes and other trimmings to be cooked up under Lauchie's guidance, once the affairs of the house were put in order. Although he had never married, his house had often been a meeting place for sessions of the Gaelic Society, for prayer gatherings from the now nearly deserted church, and for reunions and returnings that had diminished severely as the family scattered over the States and western Canada and his own generation died away. As the car had moved up the driveway Lauchie's glances had taken in every salience of his land. Now he peered apprehensively at the house as one might a loved one approaching from a long absence. The hay ran high and richly green in the fields, on toward the spruce woods behind. The grasses of the front meadow were laced with blue vetch and clover. The red trim of the windows and door had faded, awaiting the paint Lauchie never got to, but the shingles whitened in the sun and everything looked as it had when Neil last surveyed it. His uncle continued watching as Neil looped the pulling belt around Lauchie's middle and buckled it, bunching the coat like a tunic. Whenever Neil saw that coat, with its sett of green and yellow and gray, he thought of *céilidhs* and dances. It had been his uncle's private sun.

"We'll be cooler in the house," Neil said. "We're too exposed here." Sweat rolled into the creases around Lauchie's eyes. "Is something wrong?"

His uncle smiled quickly but only with his lips. "No, no . . . I don't think so."

Neil set up the wheelchair and the unmanly tugging began as he worked Lauchie toward it. The seat of his trousers was damp and dragged on the board's varnish. By the time he had his uncle secure, Neil was red in the face from trying to arrange him and keep the chair from tipping. Lauchie bore it mutely, his lips tight. Deerflies, bold in the heat, pestered them. Solitary clumps of pearl-white clouds moved slowly eastward, dimming briefly the light and heat when they crossed the sun. Neil hung the belt over the handles and then leaned into the weight of the chair. The grade was not so steep here, but he was soon gasping and his eyes danced with the strain. "Sorry, Lauchie . . . have to catch my wind." He set the brake and straightened up to rub the arch of his back. "It's not like the old days, eh . . . when we could run uphill as well as down."

His uncle nodded and turned his head to the broad meadow that sloped down to the line of poplars and spruce by the road, among them a fence of thick field-stones Lauchie had heaved into place alone. Here had been the summer races Neil remembered. He recalled them now and then in California on days when he felt deadened by the houses packed deeply around him, by the incessant traffic, by the circular routine of his life. Here Lauchie had chased horses or riled up his bull so he'd have to gun it for the fence where children waited shrieking. When Neil sprinted this long hill down to the poplars, his legs had sometimes run away from him and he had fallen, rolling and laughing through the grass. He had always thought that those days were some kind of freedom they were only beginning to know, he and his cousins, but in fact they were ending it, using it up. Lauchie had always let them win but he would show them he could run fast just the same, his strong legs flying. And he had once, on a dare, won a ribbon at the Highland Games in a neighboring county. But here he had feigned lameness the last few yards so the kids could overtake him before he reached the poplars and, if it was Neil's turn, would lightly lift him onto the wide saddle of his shoulders for a ride back to the porch. Farmers did not like the invasive poplars but Lauchie let that line of them go at the bottom of the meadow, thinning them so the hardy ones could flourish. "If there's any life in the air, they'll find it," he had said watching them from his porch. Even when the wind seemed dead, some faint current quivered in their leaves, like light in a brook.

Farther on Neil had to rest again. His heart pounded in his throat and his face was afire. Cursing his weakness he rubbed his calf where the muscle was cramping. "One more stretch, Lauchie." His uncle mumbled apologies. He had tried to help with one wheel but that only threw the chair off course. He squeezed the dead arm viciously. "No damn good at all," he whispered. Neil was sorry this part of the journey should be so arduous, that his breath labored in his uncle's ear, that he could not repay him with a clean ride to his door, as Lauchie would have done for him.

When they had nearly reached the porch his uncle raised his hand so suddenly that Neil bent forward to look at his face; he stared hard at the house and Neil followed his eyes: one of the parlor windows, now that the light struck it differently, showed a jagged black hole in its upper corner.

"The last time I was here I couldn't get close because of the rain," Neil said quietly. "John R. down the road was supposed to be looking in too, but he's been ill himself." Fear of his own guilt grew as he spotted other flaws. The screen door, its handmade frame still intact, hung crooked, the screen slashed open. High grass had hidden the floor of the porch littered with shards of glass, torn books, a broken lamp vase. The front door was ajar, a polite crack to hint what lay behind.

"Someone's been here, Neilie, and they weren't a neighbor."

"*Damn* it. I never saw this."

"Night work. Nobody near enough to see it besides, not anymore."

The back door had but one short step and Neil wheeled his uncle there. Flies played about the screen and sunlight on its mesh obscured the room. As Neil teetered him over the step and opened the door, Lauchie's shoulders slumped. Glass crunched under the wheels as they entered the kitchen. A wreck of pots and dishes and cutlery, it reminded Neil of the galley of an ore freighter he'd decked on years ago; a fierce fall storm on Lake Huron had raised a hell like this, but the young cook had expressed only relief that he'd gotten through the gale at all. But here there was something sickening in the air, something blind and stupid that made Neil's throat tighten. They had sown the floor with oatmeal and flour and soap, left the taps running and the sink plugged with a towel. Beneath a porridge of mold the linoleum had cracked and curled over bleached and warped floorboards. The taps were dry now, the pump motor burned out. The walls had been pierced with some sharp instrument from the toolshed and splattered with paint as dark and chilling as blood. The tools they hadn't wanted lay flung about—his old wooden planes, an adze, a drawknife. The pale flowered wallpaper revealed a bright new rectangle where they had ripped away the crank telephone, an old item with new value.

"*Luchd-millidh!*" his uncle said. Destroyers.

He suffered Neil to wheel him through the vandalized room as he whispered over and over, "*Tha na h-uile briste.*" Everything is broken. Not much of the furniture, built by Lauchie or his dad, had been spared. In the parlor they had used the weight of the huge family Bible to smash a small table to the floor. Framed photographs, those children he'd race and run for, were disfigured with such malice that it was frightening to imagine what kind of energy had accompanied it, what cries and looks. Neil could hear his uncle's breathing drawn out in the quiet hallway. Shouldn't he have come here and stayed until Lauchie could return? His mother had told him that break-ins and vandalism had become common in the region, that in the country no untended house was safe, yet somehow Lauchie's place seemed beyond that threat. Who could come to it to destroy?

"I can't believe this," Neil said.

"Too many in the city know the country now," his uncle murmured.

"I'll clean it, I'll fix everything, everything . . ."

His uncle reached back, took hold of Neil's hand and held it as if to quiet him. Upstairs a curtain flapped softly. "Well. . . ." Lauchie withdrew his hand and made motions of bracing up in the chair. "We'd best look outside, eh, Neilie? Can't cook haddock on a cold stove."

Neil pushed the wheelchair through the grass, his

arms rigid and trembling, while his uncle talked away as if nothing had happened. "The hay will have to dry before we cut." He pointed to areas flattened down as if a horse had rolled in them. "See there? She's lodged." They stopped at the barn and peered in the dusty windows at the tractor and baler, the remains of last year's hay in the lofts. Lauchie kept no livestock, hadn't for years, but he grew fine hay and people drove a long way to buy it. They went on to the wagon shed. Locked, nothing amiss. He'd heard that a man from Ontario had bought the old MacRae place to breed trotters. Lauchie yanked a few wisps of orchard grass from the ground and stroked their powdery tops. "No hay like this at MacRae's."

Neil ducked behind the shed to piss. He gazed around at the tall black spruce that bounded his uncle's fields. If you looked carefully, you could see their branches tinged with red. The budworms were back with a vengeance. The woods would be full of their millers now, busy with another generation the trees would feed until groves of them stood dead to the roots, their limbs gray and brittle and scabbed with lichen—a forest of ghosts. What was it that had enraged the housebreakers so? Workmanship? Love?

When Neil returned, Lauchie looked weary and shrunken in his chair. The stalks of hay he had plucked lay in his lap like an old bouquet.

"I think I'll buy me a sheltie and a little cart he can pull me around in." His voice was flat. He squinted at the house and said bitterly, "*Talla nan corn*." House of revelry.

"Lauchie, we'd better go over to Ma's now. We can call the Mounties from there."

"They won't find them. They never do. Take me out front, Neilie boy. I'm terrible tired. I want to sit awhile."

As Neil pushed his uncle back toward the driveway he told him he would start on the damage first thing tomorrow, and he'd stay until September if need be. "I'm not half the carpenter you are, but I can do a good bit. With the water pump, it's probably just the motor. . . ." But he quit. He was filling the air with prattle and Lauchie nodded almost sleepily. When he stopped the chair in front of the porch and set the brake, he saw the belt was missing. Before going back to find it, he stood with his uncle looking over the Bras d'Eau so blue in the strong afternoon light. Lazy lines of tidal drift moved toward the Atlantic, darker in the east. Gulls and terns were feeding along a white scribble of shoal. Lauchie pointed there.

"The oxen hole, Neilie."

"I remember."

Years ago a team of oxen had gone through the ice there, too thin because of currents, and were never seen again. Above it a black-backed gull, glutted with fish, lumbered into the air. Lauchie watched it rise and disappear behind the shoreline trees.

"Coffin-carriers," he said. "That's what my dad called them." The leaves of the poplars trembled like sequins in the easy wind.

"I have to track down the belt, Lauchie. We lost it somewhere."

"It could stay lost, boy, if I had my say."

"You be all right here?"

His uncle gave him a thumbs-up.

Their itinerary behind the house was not hard to trace. The chair had pressed a path through the grass and he found the belt lying in front of the barn. Wind fanned through the hay like soft fire as he stood fingering its cheap leather. Many years it had been since he'd seen these fields mowed, felt stubble under his shoes. He could not remember what they had looked like cut and still.

Returning, he caught sight of movement in the meadow. He hesitated, uncertain of what he saw: his uncle had started down the slope. Not fast, leisurely even, bumping along through the sway of the grass, and Neil was confused whether to let him go or to stop him. But as his legs began to move him toward his uncle, the wheelchair too had gathered speed, descending in earnest. Soon Lauchie was riding wildly over the uneven ground, bouncing almost comically in the seat, his bad arm leaping and waving uncontrolled. Neil ran hard for him, his mouth wide to shout. But what could he cry? Stop? Let me win? From here it looked like a joyride: Lauchie holding tight to one armrest, his body jammed down in the seat as momentum hurled him on toward the poplars. Neil, his legs already tired and stiff, lost his balance and pitched forward into the grass, rolling to a stop. He lay blinking in the sun. He did not want to get up, not this time. The blue of the sky, framed with hay, was vast and dizzying. He closed his eyes against it.

There was a gutteral yell, so brief it might have meant anything, followed by a faint crash. Then he was on his feet and trotting toward the spot where a struck branch and its torn leaves still vibrated.

Millers, disturbed by the noise, blew about the trees like dull snowflakes and then melted into the nearby spruce. As Neil stepped through the bent saplings, he saw the chair tumbled on its side, the spokes of its free wheel spinning softly, wreathed with wisps of grass and clover. A raven, catching glints of sunlight from the rim, rustled curiously in the peak of a high poplar. "*Fitheach,*" Neil said, loud. The bird flapped noisily into flight. Neil stood just inside the trees, his head raised, listening. The air was cool and moist, the earth soft with needles and moss. He heard a car on the road below: the kid was heading out again, gravel roaring under his fenders. The sound passed by and Neil hoped he would not hit the sandpipers, they were so close to the road. He could see the coat and he concentrated just on that, on the colors: that swatch of brightness, perfectly still, against the dull grey stones. He thought that this could be all of it, that time could stop in this way, holding them, and it would be a kind of winning, the suspended essence of this place he loved, death just another color in the woods. But then his uncle called out his name. Neil pushed aside the branches and crouched over him: his eyes were open and dark, angry even, and blood crept into the grey of his mustache, his chest, that great cage of withering muscle, heaving deeply for the air he was determined to have.

He gave a weak nod to the stones.

"I'm tougher than them," he said. "My heart and my head too."

"Jesus, Lauchie, I thought you were gone." Neil sat him up against the stone fence, brushed leaves from his hair. "Are you hurting? You hurt?"

"Not anymore." Lauchie reached out and yanked a pale yellow mushroom from the grey moss. "Take me up, boy. It's time to go home."

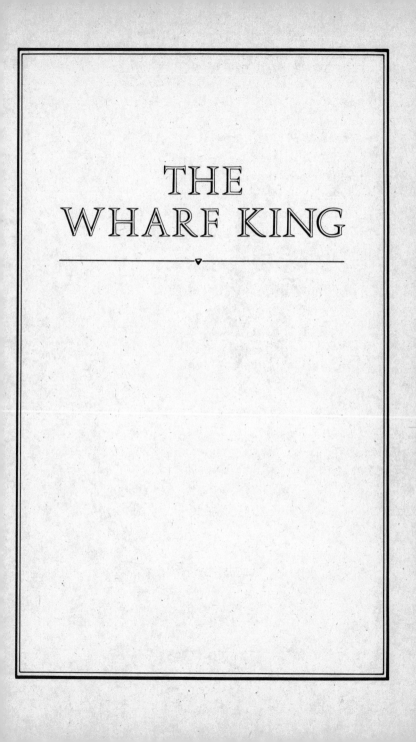

THE
WHARF KING

Graham stood at the window and listened to his mother rocking in the parlor behind him. Out across the Bras d'Eau the moon was a tattered white line on the fast running tide. No one would be rowing across those currents tonight. Now if you wanted to cross that strait you had power or you took the bridge. Further up the shore just above a line of spruce he could see a beach fire.

"Come away, Graham," his mother said, "It's no good hanging your face in the window."

"I know that, Ma."

He knew too that she was shaking her head slowly as she rocked. She was Cape Breton country, a woman who could sway there until the worst of her grief was gone, moving in that rocker like a metronome. Graham wanted to be moving too in some significant way but he did not know the right motions anymore, too many years away to be eased by rituals. At the funeral he had barely been able to follow the bit of Gaelic Scripture Reverend MacAuly had put in and he'd whispered through the hymns. But then, it had been hard to believe Rory was closed away in that casket, his once-handsome face unfit for a final look.

Graham ran his gaze along the dark ridge across the narrow strait. The day had been sultry for Cape Breton, the mourners fanning at deerflies as Rory was lowered into the clay. But a cooling night wind had risen from the west, drawing into the room the spicy sweet smell of white lilac. The darkness outside seemed to take no light at all from the moon and stars. In the distance the beach fire trembled like a match flame, just beyond it the still, white glare of the range light. Were the boys waiting? He had seen them at the funeral, diffident in their Sunday ties. They had said nothing about the usual Saturday evening at the shore, whether they hoped he would come, funeral or not. They would be near the place now where Rory had been found, his body woven up with strands of kelp and buoy line, and maybe some sticks of driftwood they were burning now.

"The boys are at the shore."

"On Saturday always," his mother said. "Rory it was they used to wait for. Now it's you." She stopped and looked at the wall for a moment. "I thought he loved me more than that," she whispered.

Graham drank the rest of the whiskey in his glass and then filled his hip flask from the bottle. His mother,

never a drinker on any occasion, had brought
from some hiding place and handed it to him without a
word. They did not hold the old-time wakes anymore,
just a remnant of them, an evening of visitors at the
funeral home. No more all-night vigils. And where in
New Skye would you go now for a fiddler, and enough
dancers to fill this room?

The rocker ticked and ticked. *"I'm afraid for Rory.
He's been living hard you know and the other night
John Willy Grant saw a forerunner, a bad light. Can
you come home for a bit? It's been so long."*

*"Dear Ma, I don't believe in forerunners and nei-
ther should you, but yes, I will come when I can. . . ."*

Graham left the house to get away from the sound.
He stood in the tall grass outside, the wind moving
through it in long sweeps, and made out the silhouette
of his car careened and derelict in the old pasture, a
dark hulk where MacAskill's tractor had towed it last
week. Rory took it without asking, more and more
often over the summer, until the night the Mounties
chased him down the New Skye road and he put himself
out like a hissing ember in the shallow waters of Mac-
Askill's pond. The car still reeked of mud. "I guess
that's your last caper for awhile," Graham had said, giving in easily to his brother. Unable to know him, it
seemed, to get into the eye of his storm, he had ignored
Rory's brazen use of the car, the creases in its fenders,
the stale liquor smell in the seats. And he lent him
money because he felt he owed something to this
brother of his, and money would do until he could figure out just what and how to give it. But Rory had one

caper left. Late at night he had rowed out into the Bras d'Eau when the tide was running like now, and a pulpwood freighter outbound from Baddeck had bashed his boat into kindling, the captain, unaware, continuing to Finland.

When Graham reached the bottom of the driveway he broke into a trot, his feet scuffling softly along the dirt road. Hardly a car would come tonight, just summer people or kids on a lark. The road was banked with tall spruce that on the seaward side listed in uneven ranks toward the strait. A recent storm had sent an old one down, its great clay ball an agony of torn roots. Soon the waters would carry it away, turn it slowly into a sleek, stripped driftlog that would roam until beached or drawn out to sea. So Rory had drifted for days in those dark waters. Graham wished they had kept him. Not even Rory in all his recklessness could have cared to be found strangled in seawrack, under a hymn of flies. "Darling Rory," Ma had said. "Your locks are nearly gone."

The whiskey burned in his gullet and Graham slowed to a walk. He was forty, after all, when a racing heart should give you pause. As a boy he had thumped barefoot down this road many times, happy enough, or so it had seemed to memory. But when a young man he'd left, like others before him, for the Great Lakes, decking on the ore boats, from which, restless, he enrolled in a college in Ohio, leaving that too, short of a degree. Then for years he had worked in one city after another, moving slowly and vaguely westward until he reached California, already ten years from home. There he stopped, got work in a personnel department, married a bank teller whom he later divorced, an act that even from that distance had shocked his mother into a year of silence, broken finally by her plea for his return. Somehow he had imagined Rory pretty much as he'd left him, a boy of fifteen with thick curly hair, strong and brash for that age, moody and loyal. And as Graham's life had begun paling into middle age, he cherished that recollection of his brother, kept it intact like a snapshot, certain still that Rory had promise, had youth. But the instant he had stepped out of his car and seen Rory shirtless on the front steps of the old house grinning around a freshly broken tooth, he realized that this man too had been living and aging these seventeen years, and that he, Graham, knew nearly nothing about that life. When that June afternoon he shook his brother's hand, as hard and segmented as the lobsters he trapped, Graham felt like a traveling salesman.

Jogging again, he passed St. David's Presbyterian Church and glanced up at its white shingles. The front window whose gray glass had this morning been warm with sun was now blinded with moonlight. In the churchyard Rory lay among others who had never left, his headstone a suffusion of flowers fragrant and white in the darkness.

The trees thinned away as Graham neared the wide cove where the wharf was. Up ahead a house, settling with age, hugged a strip between road and shore, a dim light in its cluttered window. A metal sign drooped above the door featuring a faded bottle of Orange Crush pocked with rusty stone-marks: "Grant's." He could feel right now a good round pebble in his hand. Hear it strike with a clang. John Willy's little store, he of the second sight who had preferred to sit in his back room where he wrote Gaelic songs and sang them rather than tend his counter. But it hadn't mattered either way since a long time. Graham hooded his eyes against the front door's glass: through the remnants of a Red Rose Tea decal he saw John Willy seated in the old rocker he often slept in. He seemed to be working something through his mind as he stared absently upward at millers crazed around the light, his lips murmuring. Graham tapped softly on the window. The old man beckoned him inside.

"Just saying hello, John Willy, seeing as you're awake."

"Oh, Graham, sleep comes slow, and I don't welcome it anyway." Under the bare lightbulb his face was like sea rock, hollowed in cheek and socket, his nose sharp as granite. With a nod toward the shelves and their sparse merchandise, he said what he'd been saying for years: "I don't keep nothing perishable, but if it's in a tin I might have it. . . ."

"That's okay, John Willy. Taking inventory, are you?"

John Willy looked up at him, his eyes dark and fishlike in the cataract lenses of his glasses. "It's a lament," he said huskily touching his temple. "Started coming to me this morning in church. . . ."

That morning he had seized Graham by the arm to tell him, "I know when a man's time is nearing. Forerunners, it's true," as if he were apologizing. "But I loved that lad like he was my own." Graham hoped the lament was not ready. He wanted no more of the old tongue today, putting yet further distance between him and his brother.

"My head was lively once with words," John Willy said. "And tunes to suit them." He sighed and fumbled with the glasses that fit his face as if they had washed over it and snagged there. "Now it's like tapping stone."

The stored smelled as it had when Graham was young, some amalgam of sawdust and faintly spoiling fruit, though nothing of that sort had it carried since the bridge went up over the strait, killing off the ferry and New Skye in one stroke. But John Willy had not closed the store: it simply ran down until the few wares were too old to be bought and he sat among the relics like the caretaker in a forgotten museum, composing Gaelic verse few but himself would ever sing. Behind the sticky-dust pane of a candy case there was only a box of misshapen white candles soft with another summer.

"I can't *céilidh* with you just now, John Willy. I'll be by another day when your song is done."

"Oh no common song, Graham, but *marbhrann*. I can do you the melody, for it's ancient—far, far back to the islands."

John Willy cleared his throat, cocked his head back and eased a wavering tenor, as thin as his limbs, into a song Graham's own dad had sung, half-cut and melancholy, a lament for the two sons of Big Alexander drowned off Cape Mabou over a hundred years ago. John Willy's voice fluttered brokenly, as if from some cave in a cliff, ferrying much more than the memory of

Rory Chisholm or the young fisherman dead on a Mabou shore, *Domhnull Donn nan rosq mall* . . . Donald Donn with calm eyes.

"Why did he row out that night, John Willy?" Graham said when the song ended. "Do you know?"

"Oh, he was drinking hard all this last year before you come back. I think he was just rowing like, after a good bat. No telling exactly."

"He never told me much. But what did I bring him? Two quarts of duty-free rum and a car to wreck."

"Don't be blaming yourself, Graham. Rory was wild by nature, eh? There was never nothing could hold him down." John Willy smiled. "The night he put your car in the pond, I heard them go by, right here in my chair, him and the Mounties after him. Old MacAskill's heart near went." John Willy slipped his glasses off and stared blindly into the depths of the store. "Well, he was lively, that boy, *Ruairi Dubh,* with his black curls and the dark look. Charm the eyes out of you. We thought he was blessed. He had promise, the sort most of us never had. But he ended up just getting by with his boat and the odd job. Fished when he felt like it, like your dad. You remember the day you went off to the States . . . ?"

"I remember I couldn't find him. I remember I didn't say good-bye."

"He was hiding. Not till the ferry was well out did I see him on the wharf chucking big stones down in the water, without a look your way at all." John Willy shook his head slowly. "But I seen Rory that wintry night last December, a glow all around him, trudging across the Bras d'Eau, the ice so bad it could barely support a rabbit, and him known that night to be over in the Sydney jail for fighting."

Graham slipped out quietly and ran hard down the road, not stopping until the trees gave way to the shore. He stood panting above the short bank, glad to see the boys by their beach fire. Kenny Matheson, who was looking toward the road, hailed him.

"Ahoy, b'y. Come on down!"

He climbed down the bank to the stony beach, stepping over a lobster trap that had been run up the sand. Its laths were stove, its headings choked with seaweed, torn from the bottom by the same storm that had brought Rory home.

"We got ale, Graham!" Kenny said. "Tenpenny, a whole carton of it."

"So! Been to a bootlegger."

Not old enough yet to buy in the Liquor Commission, they had acquired a stash of Graham's favorite ale from some weekend bootlegger who kept better hours and asked no questions. John Allan and Rob came up and greeted him and Rob handed him a bottle of Tenpenny. The four of them stood quietly in a little circle. Talk was not coming with its usual ease.

"Well . . . *Slainte!*" Kenny said, raising his bottle.

They repeated his toast and then drifted toward the fire. Graham gulped the cool ale, his mouth harsh with whisky. At one time Rory had brought them beer on Saturday evenings, and then, these last weeks, Graham had taken over. They were anxious to be men and there was damn all for them to do in New Skye. If they got a bit tight and silly here on the shore, at least they could walk home with nothing more to fear than church the next morning, no Mounties on their tail. John Allan, stoop-shouldered and lanky with long restless arms, had the navy in mind but whenever he spoke about it his eyes grew vague and Graham could see him living out his days sporadically employed by the Highway Department or in the woods or on someone else's lobster boat. Kenny moved quite willingly in John Allan's shadow. Lame from a childhood burn, energetic and quick with bright blue eyes, he was too slight to demand that his leg be ignored. It would keep him home. Of the three Rob had the only sure passage outward: a scholarship to Dalhousie. Quiet and reflective, he was nevertheless stout enough to take no guff about his brains, and Graham had seen him one Sunday afternoon on the wharf trim the ears off a bigmouth from Sydney Mines who found Kenny's limp hilarious.

"Ah, this is fine stuff," Graham said. "Sure beats the piss I get back home."

"Take another," Rob said. "We had you in mind in getting it."

"Thanks, men. I appreciate it."

One by one the boys sat down at the fire. Rob poked it idly with a stick. They did not know how to bring up Rory. At the funeral they had mumbled condolences to his mother, but here at the old meeting place it was different. Rory had been their man of the world. The sight of him washed up on the stones had awed them, as if he had been a seabeast, never a man at all.

Hadn't he given them their first drinks, taken them along in his fishing boat, wrestled with them, told them what he knew about women? To them he was wild and accomplished, and if he were not nearly so free or as faultless as they imagined, they would be far older before they realized it, if any but Rob realized it at all. But by the time Graham had arrived home early in the summer, Rory had begun to spin away, leaving them puzzled in his wake. His drinking had taken a hard and bitter edge and his rambling, tormented gab had baffled them. Wasn't this the Rory Chisholm their folks had first mentioned, the one with such promise, lacking only the right break to move him off into the world? Why should he mock himself now? Why should he get into fights he couldn't win and drive his friends away? And why should he row his dory into the path of a steamer?

"Where's the girls tonight, men?" A standing joke among them. The only eligible girl in New Skye was Josie Baines whose dad, a fisherman, taught her bagpipes and saw that she turned in early. Sometimes on weekends girls drove over the bridge and down to New Skye to swim in the cove, but they never stayed long enough for the boys to more than watch them. Rory had, if he were in the mood, struck up some talk with them, winking over his shoulder to John Allan or Rob who usually stayed where they were, John Allan too shy, Rob too proud. Kenny wanted none of it.

"We're hiding out," Kenny said. "They won't leave us alone. Eh, Rob?"

"That's a fact, boy."

"And Josie's practising for the Gaelic Mod," John Allan said. "Kenny listens for her every afternoon." Kenny, who admired the girl from a distance, punched him lightly on the arm. They fell quiet again. Rob popped another Tenpenny and watched the foam run down his hand.

"You men going to the Mod?"

"Jesus, half the pipers are Yanks!" Kenny said.

"Oh, we'll go over one night or other," Rob said. "Might find a couple of girls among the tourists and throw a little Gaelic at them. Some go for that."

"It's damn little I'll be throwing at them," Kenny said.

"And then what anyway? We ask them to hitchhike somewhere with us?" John Allan said.

Kenny leaned toward Graham. "Your car fixed yet?" He knew the answer, but he loved Graham's big car, luxuriating across the backseat listening to tapes Graham had brought to relieve the tedium of a transcontinental drive. That automobile was the summit of Kenny's ambition: his withered leg had no trouble with an accelerator and behind a steering wheel he looked as whole as the next man.

"No, Kenny. I haven't much heart for it."

"Aw sure. I was just curious like."

The boys swigged at their beer. John Allan let out a soft belch. "Fire's dying."

Rob got up and fetched a large piece of driftwood and laid it across the embers. The log started to smoke and they averted their faces.

"That's a damp one, Rob," Kenny said.

"It'll catch."

A bright ulcer of heat began to grow on the underside and soon a red core glowed and subsided with the wind. It had freshened from the southeast, bringing swells that washed in gentle succession over the rocky shore. Graham allowed himself to look toward that spot the sea had cleansed by now, but he could not keep from his eyes that morning he had been summoned here. The boys and the others who had gathered stood away when they saw Graham approach, his legs queerly weak, his throat so swollen he had no voice. No one spoke. He stopped a few feet from the body. He had pieced out a feature here and there among the flotsam it had gathered like a disguise, ropes and lines and seaweed, trapped gravel and sand, eelgrass, bits of shells. Crabs had taken their due, the flesh around the exposed bones of his hand ragged but bloodless. His face, at least, was buried. "Is it him?" the Mountie said. Graham was staring at a patch of bare back where the welt of an old scar cut dark across the grey and swollen skin. Yes, he nodded, and turned away. . . .

"You really think the freighter it was that got him?" Rob said, as if the boys had been debating that already. He could only see the side of Graham's face, not its expression. "Rory, I mean."

"Bits of the boat is all they found. Seems the likeliest."

"Gaw! What a way to go down!" Kenny whispered.

"A man should show a light out there," John Allan said. "Even in a dory he should show a light."

"Maybe he didn't care," Rob said.

"What do you mean?" Kenny said.

"I mean, boy, that Rory knew boats. If he couldn't keep clear of a steamer, who the devil can?"

No one replied. That side of Rory was irrelevant now. Rob took it no further.

"He was always careless," Graham said. "I guess because he always got away with it."

The boys murmured agreement. Carelessness it was. "Oh, ain't I lovely though?" he'd said to Graham only mornings ago, grinning stupidly in the mirror at the bruised bones of his face, his large eyes shiny with some hurt deeper than flesh. Over the darkness of Graham's mind now moved a game: night hockey on Mac-Askill's frozen pond, he and Rory, young yet and light but very scrappy, against the big MacDermid boys who both went away and became saltwater captains. With no moon or fire to see by they had used a flashlight for a puck, chasing over the powdery ice its pinwheeling beam that slowed to a lazy spin as they converged on it, digging and bruising, their chests heaving steam into the dark. It had been brief but intense, fighting to see who could send that light dizzying brillantly away, and soon Red Danny whacked the brightness clean out of it, the bulb sputtering like a wick and dying as they stood over it panting like ponies. Only then when their hurts and their wet clothes came home to them did Rory know he'd fallen on a skateblade and gashed his back. "Grum? I'm all sticky here, boy. . . ." And under the slanted, half-finished ceiling of the bedroom they shared Graham told him stories that night to distract the pain, the few tales that he, eight years longer in the world, had gathered, and at this moment he could not remember one of them.

"Who's king of the wharf these days?" Graham said. He was not keeping up his end of things tonight. Usually they talked and joked and he fielded questions about California prompted by pop songs and movies, cliches the press fed on like junk food.

"Me," John Allan said modestly.

"He threw off Howard Lamont. Howard's right strong but he's not quick," Kenny said, sounding like a corner man.

"Not many challengers these days?"

"No," John Allan said. "It's pretty thin."

Graham looked toward the wharf a stone's throw away. When he was thirteen the government had installed a range light on the south corner, a twelve-foot steel rod tower guyed with cables and topped with a belljar-like dome that cast a white light over the water. Apart from a navigational aid, it became for the braver kids a daring jungle-gym. During the day they climbed it to dive and gathered under it at night the way city kids hang out around streetlamps. Any wharf king worth the title had to take a header off the steel platform at the top, a gutsy plunge even if the tide was high. Rory had been barely ten when he first dived from it because there was hardly a challenge he could ever turn down. Other boys his age, after being jeered and coaxed, would content themselves to leap off as if shoved from a burning ship, but Rory stubbornly dove all arms and legs, surfacing sullen and hurt. Later, when wiry and strong enough to beat the king himself, he would flex his knees and swan outward and down, piercing the water like a stone. Graham, but a few days from leaving for the Great Lakes, had stood at the road one afternoon and watched him, thinking, well, with all that push he won't need anyone but himself to get on. . . .

Rob's log was too damp but they all sat staring while its light faded. Graham felt badly. Even the treasured beer was going warm in their hands. Funeral or not, they didn't need a drowned man at their backs and a mourning man in front of them. He wished the damn car was running. It seemed all he had to offer now.

"Would you men care for some whiskey?"

They quickened, moving closer. Kenny rubbed his hands briskly.

"Go ahead, John Allan," Graham said. "Wharf king first." Graham handed him the flask. He drank with his eyes shut and then gave a tight wheeze of pleasure: this was the real stuff. They passed it around with reverence. Kenny coughed but insisted hoarsely it was fine whiskey indeed. Swells broke over the rocks behind them.

"I think it was my Dad's, God bless him," Graham said, sniffing the mouth of the flask. "Rum was his favorite, though. 'Whiskey for weddings and funerals,' he'd say."

They were a tiny circle on the deserted shore, the fire no more than a dozing red glow at their feet. The flask went from hand to hand. Kenny sang to himself, rocking slowly to some tune he was not ready to share. With a stick Rob poked small flames from the greying log.

"Look, eh!" John Allan pointed toward the Bras d' Eau. "There!"

Out in the middle of the strait a sailboat whispered toward the sea, only her sail visible, a faint blue in the darkness. It caught for a moment the moon as it sliced that trail of light on the water, and the sail flashed like the underside of a wing, white and gliding without a sound. They watched it move away toward the Atlantic, the current conveying it out of sight.

"Some big shot from Baddeck," Kenny said after a bit, and they went back to the whiskey.

"I suppose you'll be going soon, Graham?" Rob said.

"Going . . .?"

"Back to California."

"Yes . . . I'll have to be thinking of that." In his wallet was a telegram folded away like an overdue bill. From the head of his department, it urged him in starkly simple language to bring his leave of absence to an end. He looked west toward Kelly's Mountain. Autumn was not far off. Indian summer would blaze through the birch and beech and maple, and when the winds from the sea had stripped the hardwoods they would stand grey and lacy against the deep green of spruce.

"Aw come off that," Rob was saying. John Allan lay back on the rocks with his mouth agape and his eyes rolled back to their whites until he broke into laughter, and Rob with him. Kenny had taken out his harmonica and after a few whacks on his palm he breathed sharply into a tune, the one he knew best, a hornpipe John Willy had taught him. Rob tugged at John Allan trying to make him sit up but quit in weakness and wiped his eyes on his sleeve.

"Hey!" John Allan shouted, still on his back. "Come down, Josie! Kenny's a tune for you!"

Kenny frowned and played faster. His eyes gleamed over his cupped hands and his foot beat out little explosions of cold ash on the edge of the fire.

"Blow, Kenny!" Rob shouted. He had staggered to his feet and taken on a clumsy jig. With a whoop John Allan quickly joined in. They bumped and stumbled against each other in the sandy clearing, the fire's faint light wild in their faces, their shadows a jerking dance among the rocks of the shore. Sand flew from their feet but Kenny's music drove ever ahead of them and they fell in a fit of giggling, on their knees and breathing hard as Kenny finished up and swept the harmonica from his mouth as if he had conjured it.

"Some dancers," he said. "Could be better on my bad leg."

"Aw, Rory was the dancer. Eh Graham?" Rob said, crawling to where his glasses had fallen.

"Some thought so." Was he? Yes, in his way. A few weeks ago he had danced in a fever over at the fire hall. No one had watched his feet except Graham, and who was he to tell the man he was out of step? It would take more than whisky for Graham to see himself a dancer or a diver either. As for promise, he'd never been burdened with that.

John Allan had stood up and was shadow-boxing toward the water, aiming long dramatic hooks at the sky.

"Hey Rob! Let's have a go on the wharf, boy!"

"Hell with it. All yours."

"Come on, boy! You're going off to Halifax soon! Last chance to be king."

"There's no kings around here anymore."

"Come on!"

"No."

John Allan dropped his dukes and picked up a handful of small stones, skipping them sidearm into the small, dark waves.

"Tell you what," Graham said, inspired. "I'll put up a prize."

"Prize . . .?" Kenny stashed away the harmonica he'd been polishing on his shirtfront. Graham waited until the other two boys had turned toward him, John Allan tossing the stones away and coming near the fire, now little more than winking embers.

"My car," Graham said. "When I go I'll be flying anyway. I can't face the drive again. So whoever wins tonight can have the thing. All he has to do is get it out of my sight."

Kenny let out a hoot. "You're after drinking too much, boy!"

"No. I'm serious."

Kenny got up and looked from John Allan to Rob. "Why not then?" He would have to split his loyalty, but

John Allan meant the car stayed, Rob that it would disappear down the New Skye road.

"Any more of that whiskey, Graham?" Rob said.

"A little." Rob drank off the last of it with a swift flip of his head.

"All right," he said. "One final bit of silliness."

Kenny merrily kicked sand on the fire and they all trudged over the shore with him hopping in the lead, past Adam Baines' shack where he stowed his gear, a powerful fish smell deep in its warped grey wood, his old dory hull up beside it. The short Nova Scotia season had ended and Adam had pulled his lobster traps and stacked them on end in two neat rows along the south side of the wharf, buoy markers and lines on top. As Graham passed them, bringing up the rear a little unsteadily, he noticed that many were damaged from last week's storm. A bad end to a poor season.

They assembled on the seaward ell where the wharf wrestling had always taken place, below the cold light of the tower. Graham could remember when three dozen boys and more had raised their shouts. But in those days New Skye still had many families and its depopulation had only begun.

The king and his challenger set shoes and shirts on a mooring bitt and topped them with Rob's glasses. Kenny was officiously ticking off the rules—you could trip but no punching or kicking—until Rob burst out, "We *know* all that, goddamnit!" He handed Graham his new graduation watch for safekeeping. John Allan was loosening up, flapping his arms and jumping in place while Kenny talked to him in a low voice. If Kenny had been caught between visions of roaming in an Oldsmobile and having to root inwardly against a pal, the Olds had for the present won, driving away with his guilt, tapes wailing.

"Okay . . . go!" Graham shouted.

John Allan coiled into a wrestler's crouch, feinting with hands and shoulders. Rob backed a step, and another, weaving. The wharf heaved gently underfoot as swells rolled through its shuddering piles. John Allan swept his foot at Rob's ankle, testing, and Rob lunged almost half-heartedly, bringing himself near enough to be caught with a long quick arm. John Allan tried to secure him in a headlock but Rob snaked his own arm inside and they grappled and swung about for some advantage, Rob hooking his arms around John Allan's waist until they both fell away winded. For some minutes they hand-wrestled for openings and wrenched or tired themselves out of holds, their torsos moist in the brisk wind that made them cry out when a cold spray brushed their backs. Kenny yelled and coached, trying to advise each one equally, "Get behind him, Robbie boy, no . . . aw, John Allan, you could have *lifted* him there!" Graham had felt pretty tight coming up on the wharf, flushed with the idea of their winning his car, but his mind had cleared now just watching them as they moved and strained over the rough wood of the timbers, their feet whispering. He longed to have some of it again, that energy so quickly renewed you could simply squander it. But Rob was having the harder go now, giving in sooner, pulling back. John Allan slipped and dodged and there seemed no way through his tough wiry arms. Even Rob's half-remembered judo throw misfired and John Allan tripped him sprawling over the timbers where the sea, boiling beneath, was at his ear. He stayed down on one knee gulping for breath as John Allan hung back circling him, breathing in an easy rhythm with the rolling swells and the piles that chafed and brayed with every surge. But Rob did not rise, and when John Allan, determined now, made for him, he came out of that crouch like a sprinter off the blocks and buried his shoulder in the king's midsection, heaving into him and propelling them both upward, John Allan grunting hard, his air gone, and in that brief slackening of his strength Rob pitched him free over the side of the wharf. He dropped back-first eight feet down into the dark water and hit with a deep smack, a white splash erupting around him. He surfaced quickly yelping with the sudden cold, then swam lazily, his skin flashing in the tower's thin halo of light, to the ladder on the leeward side. As he climbed the rusty rungs Kenny looked down mournfully and extended him a hand.

"That's okay, Kenny boy," John Allan said. "I'm fine."

He shook hands with Rob who assured him that he didn't want the car anyway, hadn't the money to run one. Between spasms of shivering John Allan said all he wanted was a cigarette, they'd work something out. Graham lit two Players and gave one to the deposed king.

"He can claim it whenever he likes. Be glad to see it gone."

"Aw, see how you feel in the morning, boy," Rob said.

John Allan was keen to get dry, and since they were all sobered now, the boys said goodnight and left Graham the last two bottles of ale. Rob said if Graham changed his mind, they would understand, though Kenny winced at that. Gabbing earnestly they went off down the wharf. They had plans to make, each with his ration of promise.

Graham sat on a bitt with his back to the wind. His cigarette turned quickly to ash. The bitt rocked gently under him. Lord, the old wharf needed grave repair before it broke up in a good blow. Above him he could feel the cold glare of the range light, and before he was aware of deciding anything he had unbuttoned his shirt and tugged off the western boots Rory had thought an affectation. "They wear like iron," Graham had said.

He shivered as he approached the tower with its steel frame rising to the tiny platform and the domed light. Heights he had never liked. He grasped one of the cables: the sea thrummed in it, a faint current. But he began to climb, his heart pounding in his face. He felt uneasy on the cool, damp steel of the frame. One slip and he'd skin himself good, or worse. When his chin was level with the light he looked away toward old Rachel MacLeod's house above the road. If she spread that lace curtain in her bedroom he'd make quite a sight. A forerunner for sure, she would think. But of what? He tried to gather in a good, deep, calming breath but his thumping heart kept draining it away. Very carefully he pulled himself onto the platform just wide enough for a pair of feet. He squatted there, the light vaguely warm between his knees, imagining the grotesque mask it made on his face. The tower trembled with the flex of the wharf. He held rigidly to the platform and squinted amidst the glare. This dive he would have to time, and there was the wind to consider as it dipped and played about him. He rose, so slowly it was like emerging out of earth, and spread his arms for balance, teetering a bit but calmer now. The wharf, the road, everything behind him seemed to recede. He saw clearly the country, the strait moving inland around the head where Kelly's Mountain plunged to the shore, and further west the tiny red lights of the bridge that had turned New Skye into a deadend. The moon was gone but its absence only heightened the showers of cold white stars, their brilliance cut so fine he had forgotten how they could dazzle you here, ranging deeply and complexly over the sky. But east toward the sea, mist was coming. He could sense the land as he might run his fingertips over someone he loved. This was a point to fly from, was it not? As he curled his toes against the steel of the platform's rim he thought he heard a shout somewhere, but he bent his knees slightly and swanned outward and down, hoping he was in the long clean arc that would open the water like a knife. There was a moment of being nowhere and then a cold shuddering blow consumed him in blackness, driving him deep and deeper into a music Rory too must have heard. . . .

His eyes were slits of consciousness. He remembered someone pulling and urging him toward the ladder. Though his limbs felt like rags, he'd finally climbed and hugged his way up it, then passed out, a taste of wet rust strong in his nostrils. Now there was fierce whispering over him. Rob leaned close to his face.

"Graham? You all right, boy?"

"You're dripping."

"I came back for my watch. I thought you were falling."

"Boot. I put it in my boot."

"I thinks, Jesus, he's falling but then I see it's like a dive."

Graham sat up on his elbows. His throat felt as if he'd eaten fire. His head throbbed dreamily.

"That was the whisky up there, Rob. Not me."

By stages he stood up and saw that he was naked. The dive had torn his shorts off. He dressed with deliberateness.

"Looks like we all took the plunge tonight, Rob."

"You came up okay. But your head went under."

"Thanks . . . thanks, Robbie boy. Go on now, get out of those clothes or you'll have your mother after me."

When Graham handed him the wristwatch Rob held it to his ear. Keeping it there as if its ticking were a comfort, he said simply, "Rory's gone, Graham. He really is." Then he turned and ran down the wharf, his wet shoes flapping on the timbers, scuffing then on the road that would soon take him away.

Fog was wisping through the roadside trees as Graham walked slowly toward his mother's house. The soles of his feet were sore from the climb. His neck felt sprained. He had entered the water badly after all. Ma, he hoped, would be asleep in the stilled rocker. He did not hurry. He was deeply tired but there was no end of time to cover the distance to his bed. John Willy's store was dark now. The metal sign over the door hammered softly in the wind. The fog and the trees darkened the road and he heard a high thin sound, sweetened, it seemed, by the spruce it passed through. Pipes. Who, at this hour? Not Josie. Adam it would be, her dad. Sometimes of a Saturday, late, he would take his pipes from the closet and play, walking slowly through the pasture beside his house. Not as good as he once was, Adam, but Graham could think of no other sound more suited to lament. None. Anywhere. He passed the church without looking up.

At the foot of the driveway he rested, staring up the hill at the house. The car was a dark shape like a boulder, the window of his mother's parlor still alight beyond it. In the churchyard Rory lay beside their father under the thin white birches. Tomorrow when sun warmed the fresh grave, ravens would be strutting there. And Graham would see how he felt, when he woke in the morning.

THE
CHINESE RIFLE

D. J. was never afraid of anyone. He wouldn't back down from King Kong, I remember thinking, the time we stayed with Aunt Sadie, his mother, one summer after World War II. In Boston on the way up my mother had bought me a loud sportshirt which I refused to wear in Glace Bay, a Cape Breton mining town of some size. Though only eleven, I knew that a shirt of yellow palm leaves on a sky-blue background would, along the dirt streets of the New Aberdeen Colliery, be akin to carrying a flag that said, "Please Taunt Me! Please Call Me Names!" D. J. was nineteen and had grown up in the dark company houses a short distance from the pithead. He played rugby and hockey in high school and was to me in every way a man, despite the glasses he wore. When we'd walk out in the evenings, he'd exchange remarks with hard-looking boys lounging against faded picket fences, or he'd ignore them, depending on how he felt about them. I was comfortable with him (there were names like mine in Glace Bay and a network of relatives) and he was good about conducting me around: in the tiny store across the street (no more than a converted parlor in a miner's house) we'd play the pinball machine with funny Canadian nickels, or we'd go swimming at the base of a steep cliff where sometimes the ocean foamed dangerously over the plank diving board bolted into the rock (he told me there were miners miles away out there, working deep under the sea). Our weekly showers (company houses had no bathrooms) we took at the colliers' wash house, a huge place empty of miners that time of night, their street clothing, to keep it from dust, tied on the ends of ropes and clustered high up against the ceiling as if it had risen there on its own.

But finally my mother insisted I wear the bright shirt: she knew it had been a mistake but with characteristic stubbornness she made be bear the burden. "It's a perfectly good shirt," she said, buttoning me into it, but I felt I may as well be naked. At least I wouldn't have to endure it alone. D. J. was taking us to a movie down on Commercial Street with the two-dollar bill I'd won for the best pinball score of the week and I was proud to be treating him. As we walked to the bus, he told me how his dad, a colliery mechanic, had, that afternoon, wired back together the broken peg leg of an ex-miner, how years ago the man had lost his real leg when it slipped between the spokes of a mine car wheel, the wheel tumbling him along until it twisted his limb off at the knee. "I'd rather lose my life than my leg," D. J. said, and I nodded glumly. We passed a pond layered with coal scum and I thought I might dip my shirt in it a few times or simply fall into it myself. I stayed close to my cousin as if he might diffuse the colors a bit, but only too soon I heard a shout: "Hey, Sundown!" The sharp brogue, readymade for jeering, cut deep. My face burned. Before, I had blended in and now I was being scorned, all because of a ridiculous shirt. I walked faster, hoping only to survive. But D. J. had already turned back. My tormentors—his age or older, most of them—were gathered under a tree by the roadside, cawing and hooting and bored enough on this hot summer evening to be mean just for the hell of it. I could see their lean faces in the streetlight, hands cupped to their mouths. Suddenly I heard D. J.'s voice rise above them: "You want to say that again?" he said. "You want to lose some teeth?" I was stunned. This was no D. J. I'd seen before, my congenial cousin who'd been uncondescending to me, whose mild blue eyes seemed incapable of anger. Now I envisioned this mob of boys swarming over us, ripping my foolish shirt to rags and leaving us bloodied in the dirt. Yet, there was D. J. standing in front of them, his chin out and his hands in fists, and apart from sniggers and whispers nobody ventured out of the shadows to meet him; not until we were well down the road did they dare to yell again. I knew then that D. J. already had a reputation, and that in a town of tough colliers and tough sons, he had earned it by deeds. He could, as the saying went, stand the gaff. I felt great, part of something powerful.

I thought, though how could I say for sure (who of us knows much of anything about suicide?), that Karl, D. J.'s son, had this image too of his father: a kind, soft-spoken man who nonetheless need never be menaced by anyone or anything, and from whom you yourself could take strength.

I was delighted two years later when D. J. came down from Nova Scotia to live with us in Ohio. Like other Cape Breton men, he was after work on the lake boats, decking on Great Lakes' ore freighters. My dad was a mate and helped him find a berth, and my mother boarded him as she had his older brother and three other cousins before him. When he laid up that winter and came home with my dad, it was like having a brother around. He told me about his stint as a cadet with the Mounties (he didn't like the long restriction on marrying). He made me a gift of his brown and gold rugby shirt after showing me snapshots of the pitch he'd played on in Glace Bay—a dirt field—and of his fellow players, all sporting bloody knees. There have been times I wished I still had that shirt, but when you're a kid you let things like that get away from you. Underneath his photograph in his yearbook it read: "His limbs were cast in manly mold/ For hardy sports and contests bold." He could lie flat on the floor with a tumbler of water balanced on his forehead and slowly stand up without spilling a drop. I had to get his biscuits at mealtime because his hand was too wide for the mouth of the jar. We boxed, he in a deep crouch, just parrying. We listened to Red Skelton on the radio and, being a fair mimic like my dad, I did imitations for him of the punchdrunk prizefighter and the mean little kid. When my mother was away one night, he introduced me to beer, pouring me a glass with great ceremony and making me a salami and raw onion sandwich to go with it. But then he bought himself a 1942 Buick Special with a pushbutton radio and hydramatic and I saw much less of him. He was pursuing the ladies (on certain afternoons he met a married woman in a motel), a pastime I had no sympathy with, and he would roll in late from bars. Sometimes I'd find him gruff and hungover at the kitchen table, my mother icily silent as he sipped his coffee like castor oil. But he did come to the YMCA with me one morning where we shot baskets in the old gym. In the pick-up game D. J. was keener to get us working as a team than he was to shoot his set shot. But his sharp passes and his presence made me play above my head. At home he collapsed on the couch, coughing, laughing. "I'll be sore tomorrow, boy. I'm too old for this."

But for the Korean War he was just the right age and they drafted him that spring before he could report to the Lakes. Of course, he could have returned to Glace Bay and avoided the draft altogether, but he intended to do better than the mines and a secondhand Buick. We were all concerned about him. There were stories of undertrained G. I.s being rushed into combat and prisoners shot in the back on capture or tortured in horrible cells. The Chinese had come in on the North Korean side and driven the Americans back below the 38th Parallel; *Life* magazine showed us pictures of soldiers scattered dead along frozen ditches, hands bound behind their backs. The winter war in Korea seemed particularly cruel and harsh. D. J. tore a photograph from the newspaper and pinned it up in his bedroom: a kilted Highlander, part of the British contingent, in battle dress, a dirk strapped to his leg. "I'd sign up for that outfit if I could. I wouldn't mind Korea so much, being piped into it."

He didn't need a piper. Almost from the first day of basic training he was put in charge of others, going from platoon leader to corporal in a few weeks. From there on he advanced as quickly as the army could oblige. When he came home on leave he was already a staff sergeant assigned to the engineers. We were glad because chances were he'd be serving behind the front lines. In his Eisenhower jacket and trousers bloused over his glossy combat boots he looked every inch the stripes on his sleeve. Since I was too young for his Buick, he turned it over to my sister Peggy who drove it to Cleveland where she worked. But D. J. promised me something from overseas and I knew he would come through. When he reached Korea he was a first sergeant, and a master sergeant by the end of his first year in the army.

His letters, which he signed "love and stuff," were an event for me. In his neatly slanting hand he wrote about his duties in a place called Sopa, about turning down a commission because he preferred the authority he had to that of a lowly lieutenant. He unnofficially adopted a Korean boy ("There are so many orphans around here it would make you sick"), paying for his upkeep (he was also keeping a Korean woman, I learned only later, he not wanting to scandalize my mother or his), seeing the kid was fed and clothed and went to school. I was not a little jealous since the boy was about my age, and he was there amid the dangers of war receiving favors from Master Sergeant D. J. MacKenzie while I trudged off to Park Junior High. But a letter arrived that lit up my attention: D. J. and a buddy had found two slightly damaged Chinese rifles near the front lines. He cannibalized parts from one to fix the other. "It fires fine now," he wrote, "but ammunition is hard to come by." It was earmarked for me and he would try his best to bring it home. I dreamed of that rifle, of carrying it in my hands, an amorphous weight without features or utility but yet a connection to my cousin, to a strange place and what he was doing there.

When he came home on leave a year later I was too shy and excited to meet him at the door. Home sick from school, I feigned sleep on the couch until he came into the room. Standing over me he seemed even bigger, his garrison cap cocked to the side; he'd grown a red moustache. I knew he'd moved far ahead of me and there'd be no more tricks in the kitchen or pick-up games at the Y. But there was the rifle: he held it out to me, its metal dull, the wooden stock dark and weathered. "Buried," he said, "two of them, covered with cosmilene. I don't know why they were there." It looked scarred, foreign, nothing like the hunting rifles I had seen or the ones soldiers carried in the movies. "Coming stateside," he said to my mother, "we had to exchange our clothes and there I was standing buck naked in a line holding *this*. Some thirty-day wonder tried to take it away from me but I had the papers and he finally said keep the goddamn thing." I was fascinated by the slender bayonet that folded back flush against the muzzle, unlike the kind G. I.s carried in sheaths and affixed to their rifles on command. To me, Chinese had been quiet men in silk, their hands clasped harmlessly beneath baggy sleeves. What would a Chinese sergeant yell? D. J. had filed away the identifying marks but there remained a faint ideogram or two. On the barrel I could make out a hammer and sickle and I touched it with awe: in my youth it was a symbol of evil, imbued with an almost mystical danger. That night D. J. showed me how to break the rifle down, advising me not to fire it empty because that was hard on the pin. "It kicks like a horse," he said.

In shop class at school I made a pair of wooden mounts and hung the rifle above my bed. "If that ever fell, it would kill you," my mother said, not liking guns from the start. But I had no shells for it and so she got used to seeing it on the wall. I'd take it down sometimes to show my friends. Alan up the street wore one of those gaudy silk jackets we all coveted, a fiery dragon embroidered on the back of it along with the name of his brother's unit. But it was no match for a Chinese rifle. Now we all knew about the human wave attacks used by the Chinese troops—masses of yowling men in earflapped hats and quilted clothing, surging toward you over a field of thin and crispy snow.

We heard less often from D. J. There were rumors of a truce and he thought he might stay in the army. But one cold and rainy night my sister went into a skid in his Buick, slamming into a tree at the bottom of a steep hill. Suddenly our house became a turmoil of alarm: her internal injuries were critical and threatened her life. I shuddered every time the phone rang. My mother's tears, which I had once expected might be shed over a distant D. J., were shed for my own sister, her condition immediate and close and frightening. I felt for the first time the fear of grief, as if I were becoming unmoored, growing lighter: love had weight and losing any of it could set you adrift. But after weeks in the hospital Peggy came home and recuperated in a rented hospital bed in our den. Because her pelvis had been badly fractured, her left leg would be shorter than the right. She cried over that at first, but said to me one evening as we listened to the radio: "Boys my age died in Korea, lots of them." D. J. told her to forget about the car, totalled and uninsured. "It's just a lump of metal, girl, and you're alive."

Although he was weary of Korea after the truce, he signed up for another hitch because the army promised him a transfer to Germany. He wrote to me occasionally while I was in high school and college. "I live pretty well here and I can travel, so it's not a bad life for a sergeant." He involved himself with a foster home whose orphans had been maimed or crippled in the war, taking them on excursions and being "ein Onkel." But there were hints that he was getting restless in the army. To stay in, he said, he would risk turning into a sergeant he knew, "fat and cynical, an alccholic lifer." Besides, he had been going with a German woman, Katrin. Just before he finished his tour of duty they married and I lost touch with him.

The year I left graduate school I came home to find my room done over, the rifle gone from the wall. Knowing I would never be living there again, my mother had reclaimed the bedroom. I went to the basement where the rifle lay on the toolbench, solitary in the cleared space my dad, away on the Lakes, used only in the winter. In spring, he left everything seaman-neat, racked and stowed. But the rifle was not his (he was not a hunter and owned no guns), and so he had set it out here apart as if it required some kind of decision. The cellar was damp and cobwebby, the fearful grey spiders safe for the summer in their mossy nests. The rifle had once seemed heavy, resting in my hands, but now it was light, its barrel cold in the cool basement. I aimed it at the window above the bench, at the pane dirty with rain-splashed dust, and pulled the trigger. I flinched at the pin's snap but the only kick was in my imagination: a Chinese soldier had fired this and I knew nothing at all about his mind, about what he thought when he fixed an enemy in his sights. Had he been swept along in one of those human wave attacks, running with comrades who carried not this weapon at all but maybe, as some did, only wooden rifles, their lives cheaper than guns? Did he write to a son, brother, cousin in those oddly beautiful ideograms of love and war? Did he bury it in that shell hole, or fling it away in dying? But here it was in a darkened basement in a town on the shore of Lake Erie, the butt-plate cold against my shoulder, and I knew I would never shoot it even if I had the ammunition. I pulled back the bolt and laid the rifle on the bench. I could see D. J. in Korea, scooping away the dirt with his hands, exposing maybe the stock first, the wood, or the machined gleam of the barrel, then lifting it carefully, brushing it off, sighting it into the sky. It would have smelled of the ground it came out of.

I was hired into the editorial department of a small publishing house outside of Boston. I enjoyed the work—devising and editing ESL texts—although the publisher himself seemed capricious and eccentric, the result, I was told, of his having been indulged by a wealthy aunt and of his affection for Jack Daniels. But down the road he saw big things for his small company and he urged me to be a part of it all: he found me promising. I was ambitious enough to take this to heart, and so I was busy those early years determining clear ways to present tense-aspect systems and modal auxiliaries, returning home for infrequent visits too brief to include D. J. and his wife. A quick study as a carpenter, he'd become a construction foreman with a company that built freeway bridges around Cleveland. Katrin had two miscarriages but he never mentioned them in his rare and laconic letters. Ohio was drifting away from me, and the country became enmired in a war I was too old to go to. We were beyond that sorry conflict, D. J. and I, at least directly. Viet Nam did not lay a hand on us the way World War II or Korea had: we didn't wait for telegrams, and there was no souvenir from the place I could imagine wanting. "I'm glad I'm out of it," D. J. wrote the week of the Tet Offensive, "and besides Katrin just had a boy. Some problems, but they're doing well." He asked me to be godfather, but I was about to depart for Japan and had to miss the christening. I sent Karl John a silver cup engraved with his name and the MacKenzie coat of arms.

In Tokyo I learned Japanese etiquette and landed ESL contracts that put the company, for the first time, well into the black. At a sumo match my thoughts wandered to my new cousin: would he be flower and iron like his dad? Who would he need to be afraid of? On the way back I nearly bought him a tiny Hawaiian shirt in Honolulu but ended up with one my size which I wore bravely on the street and then stuffed into my suitcase.

My father died, and then my mother, events so close together that I was still staggering a little from the first one. On a trip home to settle the estate, I roamed through the house just before it was sold, lamenting the work my dad had put into it all his winters home, soon to be lost to us. In the basement a few tools lay about but not the Chinese rifle. Somehow I wanted to see it, to recall its details. I picked up a hammer and a stray nail and drove it flush into the bench. Upstairs, bare except for some pieces of furniture nobody wanted, the rooms sat nearly blank. We had come here from Nova

Scotia, from Cape Breton, my family, all of us just before World War II. In the New Aberdeen Colliery there were still MacKenzies, and in the country my dad was from, MacLeods and Corbetts. But in this town we were extinguished. Nothing of us would remain with this place but two small, almost anonymous gravestones that would go unvisited in a burial park where no flowers were allowed.

My sister arrived and we drank instant coffee in the living room, sitting on two kitchen chairs. Our voices echoed as they had the first day we'd moved in. Peggy had divorced and was moving to Chicago. She wore a slightly elevated heel you hardly noticed when she walked. In the allocation of things she had given the Chinese rifle to D. J.

"I think he hunts, doesn't he?" she said.

"I doubt that he'd hunt with that, dear."

"Besides, he asked about it, if it was still here in the house."

I had never considered taking the rifle. It didn't seem to belong to me, and I would never bring anything down with it. Even firing it was inconceivable anymore—its sound, the notion of its bullet entering man or animal or even falling harmlessly to earth.

"Just as well D. J. has it," I said. "You're looking good, Peggy."

"I have bad headaches but apart from that. . . ." She sipped her coffee. "You're not a marrying man, I guess, John."

"Married to my work, it seems. I have what I need."

Through the stripped and yawning window I saw two black teenagers, a girl and a boy, walking the middle of the street in a way none of us, my pals and I, would have done, never with that air of possession.

"You knew D. J.'s boy had another operation on his legs."

"For what?"

"He was born with deformed legs. He's had several operations already, difficult ones. He has to recuperate for weeks and weeks in a body cast. I hear he's very brave about it."

I wrote to D. J. expressing my concern but he was vague about the matter, clearly not keen to discuss it. "He's a fine kid but he gets down on himself sometimes, naturally. It's a tough world to be lame in."

Over the following years as Karl grew up, it was my sister who kept me up to date on his struggle to keep walking. I wondered where they went off to together in that city, he and his dad. Did they play pinball somewhere? Did they swim in dangerous places? Yet on a Christmas card D. J. spoke of one day returning to Cape Breton, not to Glace Bay but somewhere in the country where our mothers were from. He didn't say why but I felt Karl had something to do with it.

Apart from holiday messages we had no contact for some years. I was senior editor at Rowland House and had long been looking forward to a partnership with the publisher, had in fact, between his more serious bouts of drinking, been encouraged in such a hope—a reward for the contracts I had brought in and the promised bonuses so long deferred, as well as for my indispensibility, my discretion. I was one of the best editors in the business now, but I was beginning to realize that I had labored too long for a man who was both blundering and lucky and who sometimes looked at me as if I were a pane of glass between him and something he desired. Behind the orderly exterior of Rowland House there was often chaos while a near-mutinous staff tried to contain his latest binge of bad decisions. But the sporadic successes of his company (we had just come out with an ESL teacher's text that would be the bible for years) only deepened his conviction that his genius had brought them about, an opinion he could charmingly project, when it mattered, to interested listeners.

While in Frankfurt that fall I heard a rumor that he intended to sell the company. I remember breaking out in a sweat and leaving the restaurant: it was like news of a family disaster—stunning, disheartening.

I flew home from Germany and confronted him on a lovely October afternoon when I could see the splendid maples turning color in the window behind his desk. I was wearing my Hawaiian shirt, its bright collar open wide against the pinstripes of a dark three-piece suit. I thought, good God, this tall, stoop-shouldered, shambling man in bluejeans and a tweed coat is only a few years my senior, but I allowed my future to be placed in his fluttering hands without any specific promises, without any legal contract or obligation, and now his word is vanishing before my eyes. He denied it at first, then, as guilt can make you do, he began to bully and rave. His eyes grew dull: I was ungrateful, disloyal, disruptive, and he could fire me on the spot. He waved his arms toward the wooden cabinet on his wall where expensive shotguns were racked. I'd always known he was a little crazy but I had ridden with that, even been amused by it at times. But now I was no longer his valued editor who brought money to his company and cleaned up his messes but just someone who might stand between him and a great deal of profit, a nuisance, dispensible. He sneered at my shirt. "Maybe there's an opening in Tonga," he said. I told him he would have to kill me before I would leave the room, that he had turned into a lower form of life. He leapt for the cabinet, pulled out a shotgun and yelled, get out, get out. I did. I wished I had the Chinese rifle right there in my hands and my madness might have matched his own. The ugliness of that scene I could never forget, and what it taught me it taught me too late. Three months afterward he sold Rowland House to a big New York publisher and all of us who worked there received a lesson in the magic of the marketplace: not only was his profit considerable, he was hired as a consultant at a high fee while his employees were set adrift without so much as severance pay. The new company offered me a position, but it meant a move to New York City to work under others, a move deeper and harder than any I'd made. I felt beaten up, but unwilling to give in. I took time off to find my way. I wanted to visit my cousin D. J., the man who had said, you want to say that again? You want to lose some teeth? And I wanted to see his son.

They lived in Lake Village, an older suburb near the shore. I was relaxed that day, released somehow as the taxi took me through the streets. What struck me about the neighborhood were the trees: tall and narrow and, considering the houses, dense, high in the air. Up above, it was like a thinned-out woods, but below, the homes were arranged conventionally along the blocks. The light that fell through the leaves that afternoon reminded me of a Sunday when I was a boy and went with a pal to see *All Quiet on the Western Front*. All day the light had been strange even though no one said much about it: it was like looking at the world through yellow cellophane and it gave me an odd feeling, as if something were wrong but the only clue was the light and no grown-ups seemed alarmed. And then the movie too was an unusual shade—not black and white but brownish—and so bleak and alien, with no speaking, just subtitles. The soldier reaching for the butterfly at the end came back to me in dreams, his cupped hands reaching out while the French sniper fixed that young German's death in his gunsights. When we came out of the movie—not like any movie I had ever seen—the sky had turned a deep amber that permeated everything with a strange dreariness, not of coming night but of something utterly unfamiliar, and now I could feel the unease around us as people stopped on the sidewalk and gestured toward the sky. On Monday a nun at my pal's school told him and his classmates that the wierd light of the day before signified that the world had started to end and that they ought to mend their ways.

Our neighbor said it was the atomic testing and that, high up, the air itself was beginning to burn. But a few days later we found out there'd been a huge forest fire in Canada and the smoke had drifted hundreds of miles, tinting the atmosphere that disquieting color, like film yellowing. This information set our world right again, but the fear and mystery never went away.

When I arrived they were gathered—all but Karl— in the backyard, Katrin, D. J., and Katrin's father visiting from Germany. "It's his last," she told me. "He's eighty and won't come again." Her eyes were a deep brown, her blonde hair cut short. She looked young but thin and nervous. D. J. was a supervisor now in the construction company, the only supervisor without a college degree, Katrin added. His build had thickened, his wavy hair gone iron grey, and there were bifocals in his glasses. But I was so pleased to see him, to hear his voice, it seemed that everything around us was dim and diffused, out of focus. From somewhere in the house a bagpipe record was playing but not loud. The father spoke no English, nor did his goddaughter who'd made the trip with him because he wasn't well, a woman in her sixties, plump and self-effacing. Her hands folded in her lap, she stayed in a chair by the fence pretending to sun herself until she rose with a smile to help in the kitchen. We sat around a small white table on the lawn and Katrin translated for Herr Schrader, but the conversation soon grew awkward, her dad speaking to me but looking at her. He wanted to place me in the family, to know how I figured in the equations D. J. had altered in

Germany. He didn't like sitting for long, Katrin explained, and soon he got up and paced the yard. He walked with a slight limp and would stop and stare into the high trees whose tops moved restlessly in the afternoon wind. "He used to be so easy to please." Katrin said. "He gets cranky now."

"He's waiting around to die," D. J. said. "I'd be cranky too."

"No, not you," I said.

The father had fought on the eastern front when already a middleaged man. Captured by the Russians in a vicious winter battle, he'd spent hard time in a p. o. w. camp. "It was terrible," Katrin said, looking at him in the corner of the yard where he stood with his hands in his pockets, his back to us. I felt I had dropped into the center of something I could not understand but that yet I needed, that in this chair under these trees, things might work out for me. I drank two German beers quickly. D. J. stood up and I knew the boy had come out of the house.

From the waist up Karl could have passed for a small, young version of his dad—his arms and chest muscular, his hair curly and dark. But his legs were withered under his jeans and bowed in at the knees. He held his back ramrod straight to counter the sway of his walk.

"Karl, meet your cousin," D. J. said. "John and me had some fun years ago."

Karl took my hand firmly. Behind his glasses he had his mother's eyes, but up close I could see some hurt there, something brightly defiant and guarded.

"You used to stay with him at home, in Glace Bay, my dad said."

"Oh, it was good there. I enjoyed just being around him. He was a tough hombre, your dad, so I always felt safe."

"Safe from what?"

I laughed. "Well, from everything that's out there, when you're a kid."

He hooked his thumbs in his jeans and waited as if for elaboration. I assumed that D. J., like any dad, had recounted exploits to his son, and he had more than a few to offer.

"D. J., remember the time you were home on leave?" I said. "You told me about the guy in your barracks, the weightlifter who was always needling you about your accent?"

"I got the drop on him is all," he said, almost shyly. He and Karl stood a few feet apart. With his thumbnail D. J. peeled the label from his bottle of lager. He sighed. "Oh, he was up in the top bunk mouthing off . . . it was dark. I just waited for his feet to hit the deck, and then. . . ."

I didn't heed his frame of mind and I pushed on, thinking Karl would like it, that we shared this much at least.

"When he was living with me, your dad went into a bar one night, all dressed up. Sportcoat, tie. On your way to a date, eh, D. J.? This guy playing pool with his buddies starts calling your dad Mr. Peepers and won't quit. D. J. thinks to hell with this and leaves, but this character follows him outside, comes running after him into the parking lot all the way to his car. Your old man finally wheels around and puts this fellow down, boom boom. Two overhand rights."

Karl glanced at his father quickly, appraisingly. "You told him that, Dad?"

D. J. shrugged. "Could be. I was young then. What's a fist good for anymore? A jerk like him would have a gun."

I almost asked him, then what would you do, but I held back. I didn't want his answer to matter.

"Karl, would you like a coke?" Katrin said.

"That's okay. I'll get it."

"Sit and talk."

"I'm fine."

As he moved off toward the back door I noticed his shirt-sleeves rolled up to his biceps. D. J. could have taught him a punch or two, I thought, with arms like that. We were all watching him.

"He's had so many operations," Katrin whispered, turning to me. "He thought they were over but he was to have another one soon. He'll be all right. He knows we love him. He knows that."

"He doesn't want it," D. J. said. 'I won't go through another one.' He's never said that before. Hell, he's the one who used to cheer *me* up."

Katrin leaned forward in her chair. "He just got his driver's license, John. The car has special controls. He looks so good in the car, doesn't he, D. J.?"

D. J. seemed to slump for a moment. "Yes, yes, he does. But driving isn't what he thought it would be."

I wanted to contribute some wisdom to this discussion of their son, but I knew almost nothing about Karl or about kids in general. In the house the bagpipe record stopped.

"D. J., do you still have that Chinese rifle, the one you brought back from Korea?"

"Sure. Peggy gave it back to me. She said you wouldn't mind, since you'd left it there."

"I thought it meant more to you, that you might want to pass it on."

"No, no. I keep it in my closet. It's all cleaned up though. You want to see it?"

"Did you hunt with it? Bring anything down?"

"I quit hunting after Karl was born. I lost my taste for it."

When he was gone into the house, Katrin said, "Karl was teased cruelly in school, you know. All the way along. So many times he'd come home and I could tell he'd been crying but he wouldn't cry in front of me. Oh, I never told D. J., never once. I was afraid he'd go after them, or their fathers. You see, he never acted tough in front of Karl, never talked about that even. He didn't want Karl to . . . to feel weak, to feel he had to be strong the way his dad was. I don't think he ever saw D. J. make a fist, let alone use it."

The goddaughter approached with a tray of sandwiches and set them in front of us. We thanked her, me in English, Katrin in German, and she smiled and stepped back like a servant. The odd light of the afternoon altered the garden, the tone of leaf and petal. the beer was strong and I drank it greedily. The treetops were dark as cut-outs against the saffron air above them. Suppose as a boy I had been lame? How would we have walked those Glace Bay streets? Cliffs would have been forbidden. The merest venture would have been dangerous and assessed by everyone. Near the fence, the goddaughter and Herr Schrader talked, their faces incomprehensible in the shade.

D. J. returned holding the rifle at his chest, not in a soldierly way but as if he had just unearthed it and together we would decide what it was. Karl came out behind him and stood watching as his father set the rifle in my lap. He had refinished the stock so that the grain shone with oil, and the polished barrel gleamed. My hands hovered over its brightness: there seemed no way to hold it properly. I sniffed the different oils, the faint scent of gunpowder that still clung to it. I wished later that I had taken the rifle up and told him, this is mine, D. J., you gave it to me, a gift from the war, and I must have it back, I want to take it away with me wherever it is I'm going, hang it on a wall where I live. But I did not. Because no consequence seemed obvious that day—for any of us—I allowed him to put it back in the closet behind his clothes. Karl said nothing, just leaned over and ran his fingers along the bayonet.

"Did your dad tell you how he brought this home?" I said. I held the rifle out to D. J. who took it and worked the bolt open and shut. "Did he tell you about the bitter cold? About how it kicked when he fired it at the sky?"

"I told him," D. J. said. "We've fired it. That's one story he knows."

And what of the other stories, the ones he *had* to know?

"Karl, sit. Please."

Despite his mother's urging, Karl would not. He said he'd like to drive his car for awhile, if it was all right.

"Don't get too tired," his father said. "Don't go too far until you're more used to it. Okay?"

"Remember your old buick, D. J.?" I said. "That was a hefty car, or Peggy wouldn't have survived. My pal Alan and I would sit in it at night and listen to that big radio, glowing there in the dark. We drank a few of your beers too, I have to confess."

"Go 'way with you, boy."

"I wasn't too sure about that first beer you poured, but it wasn't long after. Lord, you could put that stuff away."

"I prefer bourbon now. The beer is Grandpa Schrader's."

"A man I worked for once liked that kind of whisky. Me and my Budweiser he used to make fun of."

I drank off the beer in my hand and opened another. I wanted Karl to drive off in the car for awhile because what I had known with his father a long time ago I wanted to know again: a kinship I didn't have to seek or work for, it was just there, a given. That was what I needed that particular day of my life. I did not know what Karl needed, not then, I had no real idea at all. Did anyone? We had spread out so far, the family, all of us. Who would catch us as we fell?

But Karl sat down in a lawn chair, watching us as if he expected, in this little gathering of relatives, something worth the wait. I didn't know what to say to him. I was never able to chat with kids. But I felt him listening nonetheless. His father was smiling at me as he had when I mimicked characters on the radio.

"D. J., do you remember the night I scared you?"

Katrin laughed as if this were absurd. I had not recalled it myself for years until that instant. She looked over at her son. Karl had put on sunglasses for driving, so I could not read his eyes. I just wanted to keep talking. The light and the beer made me want to hold something together even though I was no longer sure what it was.

"Oh, you remember," I went on. "My mother was away, seeing dad on the boats. You were waiting to leave for the army and you came home late, a bit smashed. The house was dark as a pit because I'd turned off all the lights. But you knew I was in there and you let yourself in and came up the stairs very quietly in the dark. I was hiding behind your bedroom door I'd left partly open, but you didn't know just where I was. I heard your footsteps, real slow, in the hall. God, I was a kid, I was scared then too but I wanted to see you jump, to see you grab your heart. But you said, 'I know you're in here, John. Goddamn it, if you jump out at me I'm going to floor you. I mean it.' There was a little night-light in the baseboard, so I could see you dimly through the crack. You had your fist cocked tight and I could hear you breathing hard, like you'd been running. I knew you meant it. If I had roared or screamed, you'd have come undone. You *would* have busted my jaw. So I yelled, 'I give up!' and put on the light. When you saw me, you grinned, like you hadn't been scared at all."

"I'd forgot that," D. J. said. "I was headed for Korea. I didn't know where I was going." He stared at the ground. "You're right, John. That kind of surprise I didn't like. There was a mine explosion in Glace Bay a couple years ago. Did you know? No. 26 Colliery, ran out from the old New Aberdeen. Thirteen dead. One was a cousin of ours, you wouldn't know him I don't think. But down there you always expect some sort of disaster, and when it comes it's no terrible surprise, like it would be to us. We get older, we want to know what's in the dark. It's not something that will answer to a fist."

I didn't want to hear that, not from him, not now. I groped for a fantasy that would draw us together again: I imagined D. J. and Karl and myself taking on a bar someplace, the three of us wild, nuts, superhuman. Maybe the beer was involved somehow in the vision of it: a myth of our vanquishing, without rifles, all who would offend us, anywhere, that the mere fact of our kinship made us frenzied and invincible.

"Needles," I said. "Do you still have that phobia?" I turned to Karl. "Your dad couldn't stand the sight of a hypodermic. He'd faint. He did faint, once in a dentist's office and once in the army. Show him a needle and he was gone, boy, all two hundred pounds of him."

"Is that true, Dad?" Karl said.

"Years ago. All this was years ago. You're the man who can take the needles, eh? Are you all right? Are you going for a drive?"

His son settled back in the chair, his face turned up toward the trees.

"In a while," he said.

There was something faintly alarming in the way he lay back. "Cripple," I thought. The word tore through me. I wanted desperately to tell him something. "When I was in Glace Bay with your dad, he took me to see the pit horses. They weren't much good in the light after working in the mines for months on end, they couldn't see well. I'm not sure why but it was such a pleasure to watch them, all nicked and scarred, knowing where they'd been. They looked so peaceful that day, grazing in the pit yard while the miners were turned up for a short vacation. The horses didn't act blind. They moved about calmly but we were fascinated, your dad and I, because we knew how they lived. It must have been terrible, eh? Deep under the earth like that, never any sun, never a breeze like we're feeling now?"

"I'm not sure," Karl said.

A quiet descended around us. We seemed suspended beyond talk, there in the yard, in our places, all waiting for different things. The Chinese rifle lay on the white table beside the tray of food as if it had fallen there unnoticed. I was aware of the grandfather standing beside me, this restless man whose foot had frozen at Stalingrad. He was looking down at Karl who shaded his eyes from that light above the trees.

"*Bist du müde?*" the grandfather said to him, tenderly.

Karl did not respond at first. Then he inclined his face toward him and smiled. "*Ein wenig, Grossvater,*" he said. "A little."

OF
ONE KIND

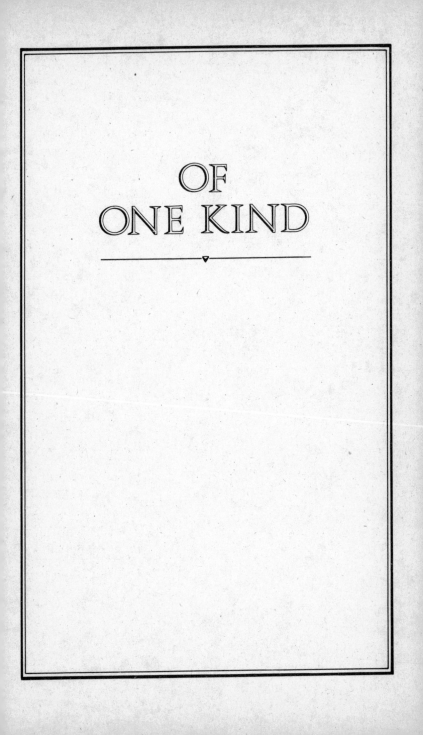

A deep voice, bursting loud from behind her screen-door, startled Red Donald, his mind still charged with the flight of a deer he'd surprised in her orchard—huffs and snorts, then the tail up stiff and white as the doe cut quickly into the woods. He turned toward the house. She was playing one of her tapes for the blind, things recorded from a New York paper or some magazine you wouldn't see in Cape Breton. He knew that, but the sound, sudden when he'd been hearing only his feet in the grass, set him back, this voice that spoke the way her dead husband had, using words like you'd wear a fine suit. Was the woman going deaf as well? He stopped to rest in her front pasture, the rifle drooping from the crook of his arm. Why should he be catching his breath now so she wouldn't hear him winded from the long climb? He was nothing to her. A handyman, a fisherman. Seventy years to her sixty-five, besides. What mattered to Mrs. MacKay except that he fix the loose board, the cracked pane, fetch her things from town? He had seen her but once, briefly, since that afternoon of her fall. And she had mentioned nothing about it, one way or the other. He took a deep breath and walked on towards the voice. The deer could wait. From the tall, swaying maple beside her stone chimney a hawk moved slowly away into the darkness of the mountain. Above the long ridge that ran as far as you could see, the day was dimming fast.

Red Donald laid his rifle and flashlight on her steps, then crossed the porch quietly and put his face to the wide bow window. There she lay on the couch, her long slender fingers tapping idly on her breast as she listened. He took in her yellow-white hair, her softly-lined face, the brown unseeing eyes. She looked the lady, even now. He liked to study her this way, brazenly, as he would never have dared before. Maybe sometime he would tell her, "I've watched you from the window, Mrs. MacKay." Let her think on that, let her wonder.

He rapped loudly. Why did she leave her door open? Indian summer was ending.

"I could've been an intruder, Mrs. MacKay," he said as he stepped inside. "Somebody bad just walking in."

She raised her head. "You're bad enough, Red Donald. I knew it was you. I know your knuckles on the wood."

He waited for an offer to sit but she lay back on her pillows. That was like her. Save her life or not, she'd make him stand there like an ox. The tape machine droned on. Someone murdered in an opera house. Or was it a story about a murder in an opera house. Probably a New York man, the man speaking.

Red Donald said, raising his voice, "I saw a hawk in your tree there. When Malcolm Gunn had this house, a hawk would keep his distance."

She raised a hand preemptorily and inclined her ear at the machine. Red Donald shrugged and looked around the large den, furnished as it had been before her husband's death. But there were bits of untidiness now: a stocking shrivelled on the rug, orange peels strewn in the cold firegrate, dropped ashes from her cigarettes everywhere. Red Donald had seen the pine panelling darken over the years, the wallpaper yellow like newspaper and stain with winter damp when she was off to Baddeck staying in the hotel. Darkening too over the big stone fireplace was the portrait of her husband, listing slightly, with his movie actor's mustache, looking the big shot he was in the New York water works. MacKay. A good name and it belonged here, but he'd been an outsider, this MacKay, a yank through and through. Red Donald turned to the door.

"Go on with your listening, Mrs. MacKay. I know how you like it."

She reached for the small table beside her and turned the voice low like someone she was unwilling to silence.

"I'm not sure you have any idea what I like, Red Donald Corbett." She sat up, touching her hip tenderly. "I look like hell. I need my hair done. But then I don't get many callers, do I?"

"I come up to see what you need, if you need anything."

"Took you long enough. Are you out jacking deer?"

"I'm going to Baddeck tomorrow." So what if he did jack a deer in the broken-down trees of her orchard? He was older now, he needed an edge.

"I hate the hunting season. I hate that first shot from the woods," she said.

"I brought you venison."

"I didn't ask for it. I wouldn't ask you to hunt down a deer for me."

"Well, the season's not come yet."

"Lean beef. That's what my doctor says and that's what I'll eat."

"I'm after losing my appetite. Could live off the skin of a snake."

The black birch cane he had given her stood against the table.

"How is the hip faring?" he said.

"Sore but mending," she said curtly, reaching for a packet of Rothman's. Proud. Too damned proud. He knew she had a bruise big as your fist, a bad sprain. He watched her fingers ferret out a wooden match. She lit a cigarette, her eyes wide, and blew out a sigh of smoke.

"Can you get me bananas?"

"If they have them. Sometimes they don't."

"I need the potassium, so the doctor says. And

since he's a nice man, I'll do as he asks."

A *nice* man, Red Donald mimicked to himself, echoing her Norwegian accent. He moved about the room touching objects with a familiarity she would not like.

"You can get earphones for them machines," he said. He had the urge to break it, stomp it into the floor.

"Why? Who hears it but me?"

He toyed with the finial of a Tiffany lamp on top of the grand piano.

"I remember when this house was boarded up," he said. "Wood over every window. Dark as the grave." He pulled the chain slowly, lighting the lamp. "Couldn't get rid of it, Malcolm. Too far from the road."

"But that's the beauty of it. And the views. I still see them in my mind."

Red Donald looked out the picture window that framed the black piano. He'd put that in for them so they could gaze at the mountain rising steeply in the near west. When he went home for the day he was done with the outdoors until morning. But his sister had died suddenly in the spring and he didn't care to sit in the house much now.

"Shouldn't be leaving your door open like that, you here alone."

"I've nothing to fear. I've heard hunters sometimes going through the grass, heard their voices. But they always go on. And sometimes kids in the summer. They drive up and shut their engines off. Then I don't hear them until they leave." She seemed to consider this for a moment, turning her face toward the window through which Red Donald had watched her. "Oh, they're just out there necking or whatever. I don't care. I envy them."

He came nearer the couch.

"Suppose you was to fall again."

"Stupid, that was. Carelessness. Never again."

Her eyes were wide and dark and behind that faint smile, he felt certain, stood the memory of that afternoon. She might have lain there for God knew how long had he not happened by and heard her calling out. Through the window he had seen her trying to raise herself off the floor. She cursed and fell back whimpering. But he had waited, feeling his mouth go dry, until she cried out again. Then he'd come inside and lifted her up, with ease, and brought her to the couch, her arms about his neck as if he might've been her husband, the man she loved. But once she was safe and seen to, he was just Red Donald again, the man who aired out her house in the spring, who freed from her chimney a trapped bird that had kept her from sleeping. Didn't she know he could have turned and walked away, left her there helpless?

"It's cold in here. I'll build you a fire," he said.

"Close the door if you're cold. I use the furnace now. I'm afraid of sparks."

"I'll watch it. I'll keep an eye on it. I'm good at that, you know."

"But you wouldn't be here to see it burn out, would you?"

Red Donald laid a hand on the cool round stones of the fireplace. He'd hauled these stones up here in his dumpcart years ago, clear up from MacDermid's shore where they rolled around like big marbles when a storm was on. Carried them in, every damn one on a hot and muggy day while her husband gave orders the way he always did those early summers they came up from New York, Red Donald doing the labor, MacKay pointing, put it here, there. But there'd been the times too when she was alone, when, wearing but a housecoat, she'd leaned near his face one morning as he showed her the rotting posts under the porch. I'll wait for the right time, he'd thought then, for to see clearly the drift of her.

"You shouldn't be smoking then," he said.

"What are you, the doctor?"

"It's fire I'm thinking about."

"Do you know what Mackay means, Red Donald? 'Son of Fire'. Charles' father told me himself. 'You're my favorite girl,' he'd say, take me on his knee."

She blew out smoke slowly, elaborately, as if to see the way it curled into the cool air of the room. A big city habit. She had a lot of them, even though she hadn't seen New York since MacKay died nine years ago. But she would speak about that city when she brought out her scrapbook. Red Donald knew its contents too well, and the stories attached to them. How she had come from Norway to study in New York, how, later in life, she had met MacKay, an older man, while working in a library. How he'd offered to take her anywhere she liked for a honeymoon. Because Cape Breton reminded her of home, they drove here, fell in love with it, bought the house for summers. Red Donald remembered the evening she appeared at his front door, tall in a dark green dress, her hair the color of wild oats. Like no woman he had ever seen, she was.

He wandered over to the piano, its surface dulled with dust, not polished and streaked with light as it had been on summer evenings when MacKay ran his fingers over the keys. The music had carried a long way then because the land was cleared and trees didn't swallow the sound. You wouldn't hear it beyond the front pasture now. Red Donald struck a black key softly, once, twice.

"What are you walking about so much for?" she said suddenly, her eyes seeking him. She had punched the recorder off. The room was hushed except for the wind hissing outside, spreading like surf through the last leaves of the maple tree.

"Seems like I have to keep moving," he said. "Can't sit around."

"You make me nervous. Have a glass of sherry."

He winced. Why the devil couldn't she keep a little rum in?

"You having it too?"

"We'll have one together. For old times."

Old times? Her sherry had been for guests and he had never been a guest. But he knew where she kept it and so ignored her instructions as he headed for the pantry and the stemmed glasses. He noticed her hands had missed a stain on the countertop and the pantry's little window was dirty as a barn's. He tucked this away in his mind. Maybe one day he would tick them off for her, shoot some holes in that stubborn self-reliance. "I rather like living alone," she said once. How could she, he'd wondered. On his way back to the den he ducked into her bedroom, a forbidden place, but ever since her blindness he'd stood and sniffed in every forbidden corner of the house. He looked at the underclothes hung on the headboard, at the dishevelled bed. Bad dreams, by the look of it. Shouldn't be rolling around in there by herself. There was a smell he could not quite place, like sweet candy . . .

"Donald?"

He returned and sat down in the big chair beside her, filled a glass and led her fingers to it. "Here you are, Mrs. MacKay. Take the chill out."

"Well, yes, that's nice," she said. She took it and sipped without waiting. He watched her purse her lips and swallow.

"Nice it is." Red Donald upended the bottle. Aw, it was sweet stuff but he guessed it would do if you swilled it enough.

"The winter will be hard, I'm thinking," he said.

"And how would you know?"

"No wasps in the ground this year. Bark is thick on the trees."

"You're awful superstitious, Red Donald, like most of your people. Narrow-minded too, a number of them."

He shut his eyes and took another swig. "And in the city their minds are wide, are they?"

"People aren't into your business there. You can't keep a secret in this place, even with the new telephones."

And what secrets did she have? He'd like to know a few of them. He knew she enjoyed the raw story, the blue joke, so his sister had told him. Worse now than ever she was, that way, Sadie had said.

"I remember the night you came here," Red Donald said. "Mr. MacKay stuck in the driveway."

She laughed, looking away toward the back of the room where the piano sat. "We were too tired to do it that night. But there was plenty of time later."

Red Donald's mind snagged on the word "it." He took a long pull of sherry.

"I guess it is you're used to a quiet life now."

"We came here for quiet, yes, we looked forward to it. But things were lively in New York, lots to do, lots to see." She pressed the side of the glass to her cheek. "You could get fed up with it, of course. But that's where the life was. Oh, yes."

"New York City," Red Donald said, as if he understood. But to him just the name reverberated with noise and danger. If he were to come at it from the sea, slowly on some windy morning, and see the skyline rise up in the distance, then he could take it. But no further. Still, that she had lived in that place gave her some advantage he could never seem to counter. "A man gets trapped in the city, all them alleys and streets and concrete."

"You have to know your way around. It's only getting from place to place, just like here."

"I'm never lost here, never in the woods even. I make my own paths if I don't like the other ones."

"I do miss the excitement of the city. Nothing like it really."

"Then why have you kept yourself here so damned many years?"

"Don't get hot, Red Donald. I stay because Charles is buried down the road. And for the beauty and serenity."

By*ooty* and se*ren*ity. He hated it when she used words that way, like she was waving a lace fan at him.

"I'll fill your glass, will I?" he said.

She raised her palm to him. "Too much of this gets my heart going."

"Aw, it's Friday. Folks are dancing. Hearts are going." He held the bottle above her glass.

"All right. One more."

He filled it and she looked over the rim of the glass. "So you've been busy?"

He let the question drift. She took him for granted, always had, expecting him one day or the other. But he'd stayed away this time and let the memory of her fall keep her company. Had she forgotten so soon? The day he had lifted her up off the floor he had just chanced to come near on his way up the mountain. Hadn't they been close for a minute or two, she against his body? She hadn't seen the heat in his face or heard the queer catch in his throat as he asked after her.

"I get busy for spells," he said. "Traps to build, things to mend."

"I was only wondering if you'd look into the attic. I've been hearing sounds up there."

He nodded at the side window where the maple's broad trunk, darker than the moonlit field behind it, moved slightly in the wind. A branch dragged over the roof like fingernails. "Could be your tree. Or ghosts, eh?"

"Another bird, if you ask me. Squirrels maybe."

"I've known ghosts to knock around."

She leaned forward, smiling. "You're serious, Red Donald, I do believe."

"Am I grinning? I've seen strange things, yes, I have, myself and others. Lights in the woods, heard sounds what shouldn't have been there. Tonight the moon's out. Fairies dance on nights like this. Up along the mountain there's a clearing. Certain nights there's a light too, and shadows moving, like dancers. Saw them, I did, and my dad too. Aw, they come back with the woods, happenings of one kind or another."

She reached out for the tape recorder and ran her fingers over it familiarly.

"Woods don't frighten me. Charles and I walked through them, often, after dark. Ghosts and fairies are in the mind, not my woods. Not my attic either."

"No," Red Donald said, pressing toward her. "Too many's after seeing them. Not the young ones, they're blind to it. But us people, yes. Now that just might be the mischief up in the attic, eh? Old Malcolm staggering around up there."

Her face tightened and she drew back against her pillows. But as if aware he was watching, she smiled.

"There's been no mischief in this house for a good while, spiritual or otherwise."

"Well, you'd want to watch out for the *Each Uisge*. Terrible bad, he is."

"Is he?" She laughed. "I've never heard of him."

"The Water-Horse. He could come up this far easy, if the woods don't put him off. A black horse, sleek, a good one you'd want to ride. You'd want to have him. But soon as your legs were 'round him you'd be stuck there fast, and he'd dash you away into the sea, down deep in the strait there where he'd devour you. Only your liver'd be left in the morning, on the shore, or a bit of your heart maybe, there on the rocks."

"My liver he's welcome to."

"Been known to come as a handsome man as well, to take a form like that, the Water-Horse."

"If I'm to be devoured down in the dark sea, give me the man then. You can keep the horse, Red Donald."

"It's not for me to say, what an *Each Uisge* does, or any of the others. You can hear him whinny in the night, that I know. Man or beast, he'd kill you."

She thrust out her glass and he poured sherry into it, holding her wrist steady.

"Your hand is cold," she said.

"Always cold where the blood don't go, eh?" he said.

Wasn't she loosening up with him now? Hadn't her husband sat like this, in this very chair, the fire crackling at his feet? Red Donald filled his cheeks with sherry, rolled it around, swallowed. He winked at Mac-Kay above the fireplace. Maybe later he'd get up and knock that picture crooked a couple more degrees.

"He liked his drink, your husband. Liked his whisky, if I remember."

"Socially," she said coolly. "Just socially." She stared into the sherry in her hand. She seemed to slip off somewhere else quite often now, as if everything was behind her eyes, not in front of them. She'd go for minutes like you were not in the room at all. Well, he could wait. His eyes drifted to a photograph framed on the wall near her couch. Before she lost her sight he had never looked at it closely but now he could study its detail freely from where he sat. She was standing on a deep lawn and glancing off to the side, her outstretched hand resting gently on the bark of a broad-trunked tree. Her hair was that rich blonde, like it used to be. In the lower corner of the print a shadow intruded. MacKay, probably, manning the camera. Red Donald wondered how that day finished out after the sun went down. Did they go inside that big brick house in the background? He could see her stepping out of the wool skirt, see her loosening the thick, coiled braid of hair in an upstairs bedroom. But the husband would be there too, standing behind her maybe, laying on her bare shoulders those thin white hands that danced over piano keys, hands that never smelled of fish and gurry. Why had she re-hung that picture near her? It used to be above the mantel with the small painting of a nude child beholding, on tiptoe, a wave breaking, delicate as china, upon her feet.

"How bad *is* your sight then?" he said with boldness that made him flush. He held his breath. She raised her chin at him.

"I'm not as blind as you think, Red Donald. I see the shape of you there. Not your details, but I know what you're like."

His cheeks felt hot. Just what did she see of him? She never looked him in the eyes anymore. He let the sherry bottle slide down between his thighs and clasped his hands behind his head, leaning back the way Mac-Kay had when he was comfortable here, she on the couch there adoring him, but upright then, clear-eyed and listening.

"Things closed in on you like, eh?" he said. He wanted to know more about her than he dared ask, more than thumbed photos and clippings in a scrapbook.

"I know what's beyond the windows. That's as clear as if I was seeing it now."

Red Donald narrowed his eyes almost sleepily but they were running from her face to her feet. Small feet, and slim ankles that suggested her hips had not always been broad.

"You're due a visit to the doctor soon, eh?" he said.

"I've already been. Last week. Sally Elliot drove me."

That stung him. In the past he had driven her. It was him she always called, just as her husband had called when his car needed hauling out of the mud, MacKay off to the side biting on his pipestem, the knees of his trousers soaked with clay where he'd fallen, shouting orders Red Donald ignored even if he understood him. Never could fix a goddamn thing, that man. Held a hammer like an ice cream cone. Red Donald had brought him a fresh eel once, a good eel big as your wrist, and the man went pale. Son of Fire? A wet wick.

"Sally's a Jesus driver," he said, swinging the bottle to his mouth.

"She drives as good as you, and a damn sight faster. Anyway, it was a new doctor, a young man. Nice man. Pakistani or something. Said I was pretty fit, all said and done." She straightened her back. "My breasts are as firm as a seventeen-year-old girl's. He told me that."

Red Donald's face burned. Christ, she was getting foolish. And what a thing for a doctor to say. If Red Donald put his hands on them, he'd tell her no lies either. He set the sherry on the floor and stood up. The room reeled under his feet.

"I'll have to use your bathroom," he said.

"Ah, you old folks. Always running to the toilet."

He glared at her, then walked away a bit unsteadily, his boots heavy on the wooden floor. The sherry had a wallop he hadn't expected. As he stood at the toilet he could look directly through the dining room to the den. She sat stiffly, poised, her glass partway to her lips. He left the door open wide, unzipped, and pissed loudly into the center of the bowl, watching her. When he was done, he zipped up his fly with a sharp rip. He watched her quickly drain her glass, pat the table for cigarettes. As he returned, she extracted a Rothman's and dangled it in the corner of her mouth. He liked that, something dangerous in that. But it was a city touch too and he felt the distance again, like someone stepping between them, someone he'd have to shove out of the way. Seeing her grope for matches, he picked them up from the floor and struck one. She shied away from the flare, then drew near it, carefully. He too leaned close.

"Can you see me now?" he said.

The match burned between them.

"Your hand is trembling. I can see that."

He touched the flame gently to the tip of the cigarette. She took a soft puff and brought it down from her mouth.

"It's a lonely time of life, this," he said, his voice low. He had taken her hand between his palms and was pressing it firmly. "I know that. I know that right enough. My sister gone. Nights like this don't you feel . . . ?"

"No," she whispered. "I can't. I don't want to be touched anymore."

"But it's me here, look at me. Me, Red Donald."

"No . . . no, I can't see you. And your hands are cold."

"Don't say it, don't tell me that. Blood's beating here, girl. Believe it now. Why do we got to freeze up just because . . . ?"

"Red Donald, what do you mean? My husband is dead."

He squeezed her fingers.

"What about the day you washed your legs at the spring, sat there with your long white legs in the water? What about the jokes, eh? The jokes!"

"Come, come, behave yourself. The sherry's talking."

"*I'm* talking. Me."

She had been afraid for a moment and he had been prepared to seize that fear, to bring it tight against him. But she withdrew her hand and he was left clasping his own, feeling the chill of them.

"That was years ago," she said. "It's not enough to tell me you were there when my legs were naked. That's no memory for me. And that spring is dry, Red Donald."

He stepped back as her hand swam over the recorder. She stabbed the on-button, catching the volume quickly and reducing it to the murmur of a man talking in another room.

"Wherever did you get an idea like that?" she said wearily, so low he could barely hear her. "Some of us don't mind being alone. Not now. Not anymore."

He put his back to her. "I'll have a look in that attic before I go."

She said nothing. He listened to her smoking, to the hiss of her breath.

"The flashlight is in the kitchen," she said.

"I don't need it. I don't want any lights."

He climbed the stairs to the dark landing and felt along the cool wall for the door, climbed the brief steps and stood in the cool sooty smell of the attic. A square of weak moonlight defined a window at the far end. He liked attics. An attic was like the ribcage of a big animal where you could hear it breathing, hear it labor through the weathers of the year. Vague, sheeted outlines of stored objects grew slowly visible. The maple branch dragged like a crippled leg overhead. He reached out and felt the clothed surface of a chest of drawers. "She don't know the woods," he said. "None of it." He lunged at the chest, wrestling it over with a thud that shook the rafters. He waited, tasting the raised dust. When his breath was calm, he went back down the steps.

She sat with the scrapbook open on her lap, its pages of mementoes smudged and askew from her stroking fingers.

"Nothing up there to worry you," he said.

"But the noise! What the devil was that?"

"Nothing there. No squirrels or birds or nothing."

"But good Lord . . . !"

"I'd say it's in your mind."

She gave him a wan smile. "All right, Red Donald. All right."

He turned to the window behind Mr. MacKay's piano, kneading his large hands, warming them, goddamn it, he couldn't warm them anymore. The trees swarming down the mountain slope seemed to rise taller with the night, the long high ridge poised like a great dark wave above the house. Had she forgotten the fall entirely, the boards under her face, the helplessness, him taking her up—not rough like he'd haul a trap or something but with gentleness there, like she was someone he cared for, lightly lifting her, just a slip of a thing really, carrying her, pale and tired, to that couch. She had feared night would come and find her still on the floor with no lamp lit, the ridge darkening, the trees going black, but no, he had brought her to her bed and set her down. . . .

"Have I showed you this one, Red Donald?" she said, almost sweetly.

He went to her and stared down at the page she had found with her fingertips, a photograph of MacKay gazing heavenward in his World War I uniform.

"And why would I care to look at a damned picture of him?" he said.

She moved on, her fingers turning and skimming a page in one motion. "I want things . . . not to change anymore." She spoke quietly, not looking at him. "I want to keep what I have."

He looked up at the ceiling and nodded dumbly. "I'll be leaving now," he said.

She closed the book and listened to him cross the room. He put his hand on the doorknob. In the pasture he'd come through, solitary trees pitched their shadows toward the house, clumps of them conspiring at the edge of the woods further back. He thought he could hear them whispering in their dark huddles. Turn your back and they'd be upon you, the devils. They had so much time on their side.

"The trees are on the march, Mrs. MacKay," he said.

"What? What are you talking about now?" She frowned, her eyes jumping wildly for something to fix on. Red Donald hummed an old hymn deep in his throat. He opened up the door.

"Aw, yes, Mrs. MacKay, they're coming up. You can't see the water at all anymore, not a patch of it. Did you know? Just a wall of trees now, moving up. Won't be long till they knock at your window."

She lay slowly back against her pillow, her eyes roaming the ceiling as if it were sky.

"Trees can be cleared away, Red Donald," she said, her voice faint. "Cut them and clear them away."

"Too many now, dear. Aw, a great many. And slash is so ugly, you know, all grey and scorched looking. It ruins the view. And don't they always march back? Woods for the Little Men? They'll be dancing out there some night. You'll hear them. And the hoofbeats. They'll drum right up to your door. You have a lot of hearing ahead of you, Mrs. MacKay."

"You, Red Donald," she whispered. "You'll be listening too."

He slammed the door as he left, but allowed himself a backward look through the window. She lay with her arms across her eyes. Even with the door closed he could hear the voice, so loud was it now. He fetched his rifle and started down the long overgrown driveway that ran like an old road through the newer woods. He switched on the flashlight but its feeble ray was no use. He didn't care about the deer. Maybe he would never shoot another, not by jacklight, not by the moon or the sun. But he stopped short, released the safety, and fired twice into the air. The shots, loud as cannon, rippled away up the mountain. He fired again, wildly, feeling a shudder in the nearby trees. They seemed so high and thick now, the trees, wind seething through their growing branches. He shivered and hurried away home, waving the flashlight like a wand.

SAILING

I tell my father to watch his step. He is ascending the small deck that leads to the wooden tub of hot water. He is nearly eighty and it is dark here under the long redwood branches. "If I can't climb this, I'd better turn in my ticket," he says. He was a seaman on the Great Lakes for forty-one years, as long as I have been living. His ticket is his masters papers. A wet February wind gusts through the limbs above us and I think of all the weather he has had in his face, the storms and the ice.

He hisses at the heat, but with a deep sigh settles slowly into the water where I am sitting. He knows he will die soon. It's the soonness I wonder about, what that knowledge does to his mind. His future is waking one morning at a time. I want to ask him about this but we have no tradition of such asking. He knows that somewhere a cold, dark wave has been rising and that it will arrive probably by night and sweep him away.

"More rain coming," he says. "It won't last." He reads the weather easily. We had a storm recently that broke up a string of days he considered weatherless, a picture book of sun and blue sky. He believes, I think, there is a connection between such days and the way I live, with no course, no destination. He was amused at how people on the street looked harried, as if the storm were not a natural occurence. By nightfall there was heavy wind and rain. Great wooshes rose up through the trees and some came down, their roots not used to such buffetting. My father paced the living room. "Look at that!" he'd say, his grin lit by lightning. The power went out. We played pinochle with two ten-cent candles burning between us while a half-cooked chicken sweated grease in the oven. "People around here never think about disaster," he said, not smugly, but just to let me know he knew the truth.

I too sailed on the Lakes. That was the closest my father and I have ever been, those years I worked my way through college decking and coalpassing on the big ore freighters. We were not such strangers then. I was moving away from him and closer to him at the same time. Because I had gone sailing we had, in the winter, things to talk about. But I left and came to live differently over the years. For him, routine is still the framework of life, a seaman's sense of work and hours. My employment is sporadic and I wake late. He rises at six-thirty and could sleep no longer unless drugged—as unlikely for him as it is likely for me. What kind of dreams does he wake from? Does he always know they are dreams or does he sometimes, for a moment, feel he has sailed over the edge of the world?

Over the Pacific in the west faint lightning trembles. I suggest we go back into the apartment but my father says no, nothing to fear from lightning like that. A soft drizzle works down through the redwood's needles and cools our faces. The air is brighter now with reflected light, like that of an overcast winter afternoon. Ivy glistens through the warm mist. My body feels torpid, weightless. I can see trees towering nearly leafless above the house like bare hedges against the sky. Trees of Heaven. Here autumn and winter merge. A few leaves still cling like snared birds. "I read somewhere people have died in these things," my father says. I assure him we are far from danger. He shrugs, rubbing water over his shoulders like liniment. He would not want to die here, unclothed like a child in a bath.

One evening we happened upon some Cape Breton fiddle music on a small FM station. My father, who was a grown man before he left that Nova Scotia island, got out of his chair and did a few soft steps, heel and toe. "Oh I used to step out with the best of them," he said. He sat down and we listened to the host of this Celtic program—a woman with Irish affections and a mind full of political mist—interview a young man who was, apparently, versed in Cape Breton folk music. But, strangled either by ignorance or stage fright, he could not locate Cape Breton very precisely. "It's west of Ireland, isn't it?" The woman said helpfully. "And east of Quebec?" After a long delay, the man said, "yes," which was true but not useful, and there Cape Breton remained. But my father enjoyed "Donald MacLean's Farewell to Oban" and "Miss Lyle's Reel." He told me suddenly about having pneumonia when he was three years old, an illness often fatal in those days, especially in the country, and how his dad made him a small wooden mallet so he could rap the headboard when he needed anything or was afraid. For the rest of the evening he was quiet.

I do things for him my mother once did, when he was home for the winter. I mix him a whisky in the afternoon and again in the evening when we talk. I bake Bisquick biscuits, cut cheese, cook, ask him if he's comfortable. I do this because he can take care of himself, not because he cannot. Around the corner from us there is a convalescent home and his first day here my father saw a frail old man babystepping by our window with a walker. I had to smile when he said, with real sympathy, "Poor old fella," as if there were years between them. Last night, halfway through his second whisky and feeling good, he remembered a country party ("Long before *I* was married"), a wedding reception back in Cape Breton. A lot of people came to this cold house on Cape Dauphin, stamping snow at the door, December be damned, and there was dancing and boozing, horses packed flank to flank in the barn. A pal of his got sick from drink, but before going upstairs to find a bed he searched around the yard in the dark, finally yanking out of the snow an enamel creamer to set by his bedside. Not until morning, after he'd thrown up in it twice, did he discover the bottom of the creamer was rusted out completely. My father likes reminiscences like this and laughs easily, shaking his head at how vivid they remain. But after the funny part he said, almost casually, "Your mother was there," and the timbre of his voice changed, just slightly, just enough to notice.

I remember one December when I waited with my mother at a Cleveland dock during a bleary hour of the morning and watched his ship ease like an iceberg into her moorings. Freighted with tons of ice, she had gone down dangerously on her marks because of the added burden. My mother knew about the storm and had been worried. My father, bundled up like an Arctic explorer, waved to her from the Texas deck and she gave him the okay sign. Later that winter, at home, my father and I walked along the shore of Lake Erie, our eyes and mouth drawn tight against a wind so cold it pained. We squinted across a jagged icescape which, rough as rockslides and fluted with windrows of snow, had been repeatedly broken up by storms, freezing again and again into new shapes. Beyond it the water seemed calm and green in the distance. We passed a shed built along the lines of a little house and layered with several inches of translucent ice. Beside it a tree crackled, wind-driven spray having turned it as bright and brittle as crystal. Too chilled to bring a hand out of his pocket, my father nodded toward the shed. "Somebody forgot to keep the home fires burning, eh?" he said. He and my mother argued sometimes during the long winter months. She accumulated grievances in her loneliness and sometimes shut herself away in her room after he left. What they quarrelled about I cannot recall.

Little things which, I suppose, the strains of separation made larger. It no longer matters, not to him, not to anything. Soon his voice will stop and there will be nothing more he can add to what I know of him. We walked in the wind that day until we could barely speak.

"In a ship," he says, "out there at night . . . it's sometimes like you're at dead center of everything, the works." There are breaks in the overcast now. Clouds tear slowly into pieces and drift off like floes in the dark sky. My father watches them, then points. "The brightest star, there. Sirius. And there, Eye of Taurus." Wherever I am, he has told me, I like to get a bearing. All I know about him are bits and pieces like this. He never talks about himself directly, never did. He prefers stories that entertain—anecdotes, mimicry. Some stories I have heard before, like familiar waters we sail over. I wish we could descend beneath them, that he could reveal things under the surface before it is too late. When he is feeling down he is merely politely silent. Yet I admire his reticence: it seems dignified in a land of public blubbering where people yearn to be heard. At my mother's sudden death a year ago he was, as I expected, stoic, although the shock of her absence had tightened his face. She died next to him in bed, on a normal morning when he rose early and waited for her to come down to breakfast. When he looked at the clock later on, an ordinary day turned into something vaguely expected but never prepared for. "I climbed those stairs like I weighed a ton," he told me. She was already blue and cold. It troubles him that he did not become alarmed sooner, that he might have reached her in time.

The first night he arrived I passed his room and was struck to see him down on one knee beside his bed, whispering prayer. I had forgotten he prayed that way and I was briefly embarrassed, as if this was senility. No. Like other things about him, it is simple and private, as sincere as a Jew at the Wailing Wall or a Moslem on his mat. I wondered if he had prayed beside his bunk when he was a deckhand, how he found the chance or if he feared the jibes of his shipmates. What now does he ask for? What does he expect from God?

He has marvelled at the flowers in February. He left the sidewalk one morning to stand among the branches of a tulip tree and touch the pale lavender cups of its blossoms. "You live in a garden," he said. At home he took over my mother's roses and put in peonies of his own, and marigolds. A sudden show of flowers makes him smile, almost shyly. He missed so many summers at sea, and they seem to strike at the heart of his youth when he knew them in the country.

Yesterday we were hit with an earthquake. Still in bed, I woke certain that this was the Big One and I did not want to meet it hungover and naked. I stumbled to the doorway of the living room where a hanging fern swung like a pendulum. My father, half-crouched in front of his chair, had spread his arms like a wrestler—a reflex from years of steadying himself on pitching decks. We stayed as we were, our eyes fixed on each other, until the rolling passed and the house stopped shaking. At the front window my father looked down at the street, his face close to the glass as if he were back in a wheelhouse. "Not the same as a ship," he said. "It's like being thrown off the earth." Then he smiled and raised his voice like a preacher's: " 'If I take up the wings of the morning, and dwell in the uttermost part of the sea. . . .' " He lowered his voice to a murmur, " '. . . even there. . . .' "

The moon appears in the southwest. Its light turns the water darkly clear, the way it might be on Lake Superior streaming out a deep green against a wake white and crisp. We can see the pallor of our skin. My father sighs, a habit of his now, though usually no words ever follow. The last months his wife was living she would not enter a dark room. At the threshold she would step back and wait while he went ahead of her and put on a light. At the funeral he looked at her in that casket for a long while, and finally he said, to no one: "Where is she *now*?" I was of no use to him in this matter. I do not know how we move after death, or where.

In our old neighborhood back home five widows have been good to him. They observed his birthday, they bring him meals, invite him to their houses for cards. One has taken to calling him dear, a familiarity he does not encourage. He has named her The Star Widow, but when she calls him darling, he says, he will have to cool her off. "I have old feelings to think about. I don't need any new ones." After my mother died, he burned her letters. My anger puzzled him. "Letters are for the living," he said.

In the Twenties my father wheeled on a small Canadian freighter whose captain, a reckless alcoholic, took her foolishly into a Lake Michigan storm. Her wooden hatches, weakened by boarding seas, were carried away and she soon foundered. He and three other men made it to the wooden raft lashed atop the wheelhouse. All night in the darkness they were swept from it time after time, clawing their way back aboard where they huddled like lovers in the cold. It was November and the water was not much above freezing. A man would stop talking for awhile and then he wasn't there, having slipped quietly into the sea. By dawn when the wind had abated, only my father remained, half-conscious and hallucinating. A bearded man kept appearing on the edge of the raft warning him not to eat the ice he'd been nibbling from the lapels of his coat. He heard his dead shipmates calling to him from shore offering him sandwiches. "Go easy, I'm not dead," he said to the Coast Guardsman who'd lifted him like a corpse. He lost two toes and the tip of a finger. "I survived," he told me, "because I was young."

Vapor rises faintly through the moonlight, climbing into the boughs above us whose shadows flash in the steam. I see my father's spare gestures, his pale form. And the occasional spark of his gold tooth, quick as an atom, so contained it seems all I know of him, that tiny glint. He bought that tooth in his bold and single days, just after lay-up, a bonus in his pocket and an aching bicuspid cracked in a fight with a redneck oiler. It always embarrassed my mother, fearful he would grin in church or pick it in a good restaurant. But I like it because it reminds me of his youth about which I know little. In Gaelic, a language his parents spoke, his name means sailor or mariner. As he grew up, I guess he merely eased into what he'd been christened, and that was his life.

We have been up to San Francisco once during his visit. He likes to call it Frisco, a city he has always wanted to see. Indifferent to cities, I take us on a sketchy itinerary of sights. I look for a Scottish bar I've heard about but we soon end up, by mutual consent, in a dark Irish pub where we talk quietly in the cool malty dusk of our Guinness. Outside, people hurry past in the sun. We swap stories about the Lakes, boats we both knew, men we'd worked with, as if we're ashore for a few hours while our ships unload. Later, reluctantly, we stumble out into the glare of the afternoon in time to board the ships docked at the Maritime Museum. We clamber around an old steam schooner, the sort of working ship my father understand immediately. In the fo'c'sle he sniffs a tarry smell. "Oakum," he says, grinning back to that tooth that can still surprise me. We inspect every accessible compartment and only the wheelhouse remains. It is perched high and solitary like the wheelhouses on the old Lake freighters that are no doubt gone by now. We climb to it but the door is locked. No public permitted. My father peers through the glass for awhile, hooding his eyes and cataloging the equipment inside. Then he turns and I snap a picture of him looking older in the cold wind. We hang around the piers. I know he doesn't want to leave. He sees a sloop plunging through the choppy currents off Alcatraz Island and tells me about a skiff he had as a boy, how he rigged a little sail and put rocks in the bottom for ballast. As we drive home, the Guinness seeps ruthlessly from our spirits and I recall how harshly the sun struck us when we stepped into it. We are silent all down the Bayshore where nothing generates talk. I turn on the radio. On our little FM station Pete Seeger is singing . . . "Sailing down my golden river, and I was not far from home. . . ." I look over at my father. He seems dozy. Perhaps his thoughts are somewhere on water, on the cold dark sea of Lake Superior.

He makes swimming motions with his hands. The water ripples and whitens behind him. I remember only one summer when he swam. His boat laid up because of a steel strike and in the afternoons we would catch a bus down to the lake. He would swim out a long way by himself, slowly and carefully, where there were no other swimmers and float for minutes on end, his face a mask on the water. I was too young to follow him, but I knew, anyway, he wanted to be alone. Summer at home was a strange time for him.

He knows that I am still drifting. "A man needs some place to tie up to," he said in the Irish pub. It troubles him that I have lived in so many places, that next year I may have another address. Quite likely it will not have this warm bubbling sea in the backyard. I work on and off as a construction laborer. I dig, fetch, bang nails out of boards, clean up after insolent young carpenters who have seen themselves in too many beer commercials. I don't know where this will lead. In the spring my father was always gone as soon as the ice broke. A different ship but the same places. "Never mind," he told me, wiping Guinness froth from his moustache. "The company gave boats to younger mates and put me mate with them so they wouldn't screw up. I never got my own ship. You had to kiss their ass for that." He looked across the bar at a woman in a slit skirt. "I was into my middle years when you came along, Danny." He kept looking at the woman and nodding his head as if considering what my coming along had meant. Finally he said, "Just don't have anything to do with business. It's not in our blood." We touched glasses and finished our Guinness.

Once a bunkmate and I devised a game. Running up Lake Superior in hard weather, we opened the porthole in our cramped, below-decks cabin and climbed into our bunks. We lay there naked and uncovered, rigid as mummies, listening to the bow smash and split the heavy seas. Which of us would feel the first fiery lash of water so cold it could kill you in minutes? We heard the seas break along the shipside, rise to the porthole's rim, splattering the top of our metal dresser, and we knew that inevitably a good wave would collide with the bow and swell upward. We tensed, our jaws clamped tight. Soon there was the sound—a growing hiss, a roaring whisper—and then a thump of spray shot through the darkness, striking one or both of us with a chill that jerked the body like an electric shock. Whoever yelled first lost. We played until wet bedclothes threatened our sleep. I thought of my father on that raft, that I was he. But I did not think of death: death was too distant, like the bottom of that dark sea two hundred fathoms beneath us, so cold it never gave up the drowned men who drifted there. As I closed the porthole, I was sure I would live forever.

"Too hot," my father says. He rises, emerges from the water. I reach out a steadying hand he does not need. He towels himself slowly, in that careful way of old men, as if briskness would be unseemly. He was never a big man but now he has diminished into age. I think of the only time I saw him in the act of his work. Our ships had tied up at adjacent docks in Toledo and I could see him stepping smartly along the main deck over hatch cables and dock wallopers' shovels to chew out a crewman for fouling a winch. I was surprised: he seemed such a different man, one a gold tooth might well belong to. I envied him. No one on that ship would question anything he said, and I hoped that one day I could gain that kind of respect. But I will always somehow remain an amateur. I have been an amateur in nearly everything of my life, and I am one now. Everything in my mind and in my hands seems uncertain, half-formed. But my father was a professional, skilled in those countless ways that make good seamen, and bring them other good seamen's respect. That part of him was not passed on to me, that ability to find your way, deeply, into what you are good at. When I first went sailing, I knew the ore frighters, having as a boy roamed their cold iron darkness during winter lay-up, but I did not know their work. I felt homesick and inept. But for my father, I tried at least to be a reliable deckhand, for that would get back to him. What didn't get back was the hot summer night I got thoroughly and limply drunk on cognac, me and the other two deckhands, cleaning up ore leavings deep in the cargo holds. Between alcoholic fits of energy, we leaned on our shovels and sang. We dodged the backing bulldozer and the first mate's glances from the hatches above, we flirted with the Hewlett's big iron teeth as its shadow descended over us. When the heat and the cognac struck home around two a. m., I crawled along the side-tanks all the way to my bunk and passed out. As penance, the mate put me to work at sunrise hauling up five-gallon buckets of heavy red mud and dumping them overboard. I felt sick enough to die. I hated every motion of the ship and the dull line of the horizon. I wanted to jump at the next port. But I endured it and said nothing because of the watchman. His name was Gunderson, an ex-gunners mate with bleeding ulcers, huge hands, a frightening set of false teeth, and identical square-riggers tatooed on both wrists. He came up to me while I was waiting for my bucket to be filled in the hold below. I must have looked grey as the sea, my jaws tight with nausea. "You know," he said, "I been with some sons of bitches, but your old man is a fine mate. He was a deckhand once too." I could have told him, no, he wasn't, they made him a wheelsman right off when he said he'd been a seaman in Nova Scotia, he never had to do this. But I was grateful to Anders Gunderson. I knew then that to feel homesick was foolish, that I was not in a strange place.

I will never forget a photograph my father gave me when I was young. He proferred it without comment one evening after I had pressed him for details about his shipwreck. I took the old clipping to my room where I pored over it more keenly than the pornographic cards we passed around at school. Something in its atmosphere I could not understand, cannot yet. The corpses of nine seamen are laid out in a morgue, the undertaker in his galluses posing at one end of them, his assistant at the other. A railroad ferry had sunk in December during one of Lake Erie's fearsome gales, and these men, the only crewmen ever found, had frozen solid as stone in a battered lifeboat. Their faces, grotesquely calm, skin like putty in the incandescent glare of floodlamps, have been shaped by the mortician into the contours of troubled sleep. For the benefit of cameras they lie in a parallel row, heads slightly raised on makeshift pillows, sheets pulled snug to their chins. You can see the outlines of their arms folded across their waists. But something disturbs the almost Victorian dignity of their arrangement: there is one man, Smith the cook, whose belly is so swollen its girth has lifted the hem of the sheet, exposing the deadwhite flesh of his buttock. It is clear that all of these men are naked. A copy editor has crudely penned on each sheet the surname of each man. My eyes went slowly up and down that row so many times the order of their names became a kind of poetry. Steele. Shank. Allen. Smith. Ray. Hart. Thomas. Hines. Squars. What my father wanted me to learn from this stark picture I do not know. If he wanted me only to remember it, I have.

My father has dried himself and wrapped a big white towel around him toga-like. "At home there's ice now," he says. "Clear across to Canada." He waves. I

FOR THE BEST IN PAPERBACKS, LOOK FOR THE

In every corner of the world, on every subject under the sun, Penguin represents quality and variety—the very best in publishing today.

For complete information about books available from Penguin—including Pelicans, Puffins, Peregrines, and Penguin Classics—and how to order them, write to us at the appropriate address below. Please note that for copyright reasons the selection of books varies from country to country.

In the United Kingdom: For a complete list of books available from Penguin in the U.K., please write to *Dept E.P., Penguin Books Ltd, Harmondsworth, Middlesex, UB7 0DA*.

In the United States: For a complete list of books available from Penguin in the U.S., please write to *Dept BA, Penguin*, Box 120, Bergenfield, New Jersey 07621-0120.

In Canada: For a complete list of books available from Penguin in Canada, please write to *Penguin Books Ltd, 2801 John Street, Markham, Ontario L3R 1B4*.

In Australia: For a complete list of books available from Penguin in Australia, please write to the *Marketing Department, Penguin Books Ltd, P.O. Box 257, Ringwood, Victoria 3134*.

In New Zealand: For a complete list of books available from Penguin in New Zealand, please write to the *Marketing Department, Penguin Books (NZ) Ltd, Private Bag, Takapuna, Auckland 9*.

In India: For a complete list of books available from Penguin, please write to *Penguin Overseas Ltd, 706 Eros Apartments, 56 Nehru Place, New Delhi, 110019*.

In Holland: For a complete list of books available from Penguin in Holland, please write to *Penguin Books Nederland B.V., Postbus 195, NL-1380AD Weesp, Netherlands*.

In Germany: For a complete list of books available from Penguin, please write to *Penguin Books Ltd, Friedrichstrasse 10-12, D-6000 Frankfurt Main I, Federal Republic of Germany*.

In Spain: For a complete list of books available from Penguin in Spain, please write to *Longman, Penguin España, Calle San Nicolas 15, E-28013 Madrid, Spain*.

In Japan: For a complete list of books available from Penguin in Japan, please write to *Longman Penguin Japan Co Ltd, Yamaguchi Building, 2-12-9 Kanda Jimbocho, Chiyoda-Ku, Tokyo 101, Japan*.

FOR THE BEST IN PAPERBACKS, LOOK FOR THE 🐧

FOR THE BEST IN PAPERBACKS, LOOK FOR THE 🐧

☐ **THE ELIZABETH STORIES**
   Isabel Huggan

Smart, stubborn, shy, and giving, Elizabeth discovers all the miseries, and some of the wonders, of childhood. These delightful stories, showing her steely determination throughout a series of disasters and misunderstandings, remind us that if growing up is hard, it can also be hilarious.

"Twists and rings in the mind like a particularly satisfying and disruptive novel" — *The New York Times Book Review*

184 pages   ISBN: 0-14-010199-3   **$6.95**

☐ **FOE**
   J. M. Coetzee

In this brilliant reshaping of Defoe's classic tale of Robinson Crusoe and his mute slave Friday, J. M. Coetzee explores the relationships between speech and silence, master and slave, sanity and madness.

"Marvelous intricacy and almost overwhelming power . . . *Foe* is a small miracle of a book." — *Washington Post Book World*

158 pages   ISBN: 0-14-009623-X   **$6.95**

☐ **1982 JANINE**
   Alasdair Gray

Set inside the head of an aging, divorced, insomniac supervisor of security installations who hits the bottle in the bedroom of a small Scottish hotel, *1982 Janine* is a sadomasochistic, fetishistic fantasy.

"*1982 Janine* has a verbal energy, an intensity of vision that has mostly been missing from the English novel since D. H. Lawrence." — *The New York Times*

346 pages   ISBN: 0-14-007110-5   **$6.95**

☐ **THE BAY OF NOON**
   Shirley Hazzard

An Englishwoman working in Naples, young Jenny has no friends, only a letter of introduction—a letter that leads her to a beautiful writer, a famous Roman film director, a Scottish marine biologist, and ultimately to a new life.

"Drawn so perfectly that it seems to breathe" — *The New York Times Book Review*

154 pages   ISBN: 0-14-010450-X   **$6.95**

☐ **THE WELL**
   Elizabeth Jolley

Against the stark beauty of the Australian farmlands, Elizabeth Jolley paints the portrait of an eccentric, affectionate relationship between two women—Hester, a lonely spinster, and Katherine, a young orphan. Their simple, satisfyingly pleasant life is nearly perfect until a dark stranger invades their world in a most horrifying way.

"An exquisite story . . . Jolley [has] a wonderful ear, [and] an elegant and compassionate voice." — *The New York Times Book Review*

176 pages   ISBN: 0-14-008901-2   **$6.95**

FOR THE BEST IN PAPERBACKS, LOOK FOR THE 🐧

☐ **THE NEWS FROM IRELAND**
   William Trevor

This major collection of short stories once again shows Trevor's extraordinary power. In the title story, his evocation of the anguished relations of an Anglo-Irish family through several generations approaches the dramatic and forceful effect of a full novel.

"Trevor is perhaps the finest short story writer in the English language." — *Vanity Fair*   286 pages   ISBN: 0-14-008857-1   **$6.95**

☐ **THE SHRAPNEL ACADEMY**
   Fay Weldon

At a military school named for the inventor of the exploding cannonball, perhaps it should come as no surprise when the annual Eve-of-Waterloo dinner, for which the guest list includes a young weapons salesman and a reporter for a feminist newspaper, hilariously and spontaneously combusts.

"This is Fay Weldon's funniest novel . . . an original, unconventional comedy."
— *San Francisco Chronicle*
                         186 pages   ISBN: 0-14-009746-5   **$6.95**

☐ **SAINTS AND STRANGERS**
   Angela Carter

In eight dazzling, spellbinding stories, Angela Carter draws on familiar themes and tales—Peter and the Wolf, Lizzie Borden, *A Midsummer Night's Dream*— and transforms them into enchanting, sophisticated, and often erotic reading for modern adults.

"Whimsical, mischievous, and able to work magic . . . Carter's stories disorient and delight." — *Philadelphia Inquirer*
                         126 pages   ISBN: 0-14-008973-X   **$5.95**

☐ **IN THE SKIN OF A LION**
   Michael Ondaatje

Through intensely visual images and surreal, dreamlike episodes, Michael Ondaatje spins a powerful tale of fabulous adventure and exquisite sensuality set against the bridges, waterways, and tunnels of 1920s Toronto.

"A brilliantly imaginative blend of history, lore, passion, and poetry" — Russell Banks   244 pages   ISBN: 0-14-011309-6   **$7.95**

☐ **THE GUIDE: A NOVEL**
   R. K. Narayan

Raju was once India's most corrupt tourist guide; now, after a peasant mistakes him for a holy man, he gradually begins to play the part. He succeeds so well that God himself intervenes to put Raju's new holiness to the test.

"A brilliant accomplishment" — *The New York Times Book Review*
                         220 pages   ISBN: 0-14-009657-4   **$5.95**